Taken By The Ripper

Taken By The Ripper

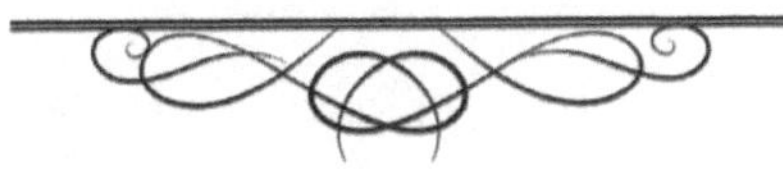

Sydney Winward

This is a work of fiction. Names, characters, places, and incidents are either the product of the author's imagination or are used fictitiously, and any resemblance to actual persons living or dead, business establishments, events, or locales, is entirely coincidental.

Taken by the Ripper

A Time for Monsters Multi-Author Series

Cover Art by Kit Fox

Paperback ISBN 978-1-960461-24-7

For those who love mystery, paranormal, and a little bit of darkness

BOOKS BY SYDNEY WINWARD

The Bloodborn Series

Bloodborn

Bloodbond

Bloodscourge

Bloodbane

Bloodcurse

Bloodheir

Letters to Love Series

Yours, Sterling

Forever, Mirabelle

Always, Ivette

Charles, With Love

Adoringly, Edward

Sunlight and Shadows Series

A Breath of Sunlight

A Taste of Shadows

A Glimpse of Music

A Kiss of Embers

A Balm of Healing

A Weave of Starlight

Novellas

Venom Kissed

Through Wylder Meadows

Root Brew Float

On Silver Wings

Bloodmoon

Selkie

A Wingless Hope

Taken by the Ripper

Chapter One

London, England 1888

Clara Thompson was one of the lucky ones. She made sure to remind herself of it every day, especially when her eyes drooped, her back ached, and her feet screamed for a rest. But at least she had a place to call home, and she didn't have to turn to the streets for a source of income like many others she knew.

She blew a strand of golden copper hair out of her light gray eyes as she bent over a patient—a young girl at the age of ten—sporting blistering scabs across her skin. Heat emanated from her frail body, her face flushed red.

Using a wooden stick, she pressed it against the girl's tongue, only to find red spots dotting her mouth.

Smallpox.

"You can get through this," she urged her newest patient, but the girl only blinked sluggishly. "My mother and I caught the disease years ago." She dipped her wash rag into a bowl of cool water and placed it against the girl's forehead. "My mother was left weak after giving birth to my youngest sister, Norma. She didn't make it, but I did. And you can, too."

A pang of regret echoed in the chambers of her heart at the thought of her mother. She'd caught smallpox only weeks after delivering Norma and managed to spread it to Clara. Her father, a doctor at the time, had quarantined them together, separating her from her sisters. Those were grueling days of her father trying to keep baby Norma fed while separating infant from mother. And poor little Mazie, her four-year-old sister at the time, hadn't quite understood why her life had drastically changed, especially when their mother had succumbed to death.

A knock at the door startled her upright, and her gaze shot toward the sound.

"Clara, it happened again!" Mazie shouted through the door. "Come see!"

"Step away!" Clara warned, crossing the quarantined room in several strides over creaky wooden floorboards. "You know you are not allowed near this room." Not when her sisters had never been exposed to smallpox before.

"But the Whitechapel Murderer has struck again!"

Everything else shamefully fled from her mind as she vigorously scrubbed her hands in the basin beside the door, barely managing to dry them in her haste, and slipped into the hallway.

Sure enough, Mazie held *The Star* newspaper in her hands, the pages rattling in tune with her excitement. "Here it says they found her in an alleyway with her throat slit. But something wasn't quite right about the body. They're saying the murderer is mimicking an animal attack. But the wounds were so precise that it couldn't be an animal at all."

When her sister's trembling hands shook the newspaper enough to blur the words, Clara snatched the periodical from her and peered at the article in her own steady hands. Her eyes flew across the page, jumping from line to line as she read the details of the most recent murder. Another woman. A prostitute, just like the last victim.

"They are calling him Jack the Ripper now," Clara murmured, brushing her thumb along the ominous name.

"You don't suppose his name is actually Jack, do you?"

She gave her younger sister a pointed look, one similar to her father's disbelieving stare when one of them had said something foolish. "It's just an alias, Mazie. Besides, you should not concern yourself with such matters. This is not exciting. It's *horrifying*."

She shouldered her way past Mazie and snatched a pad of notes from a nearby table, reviewing the symptoms of her patients as she made her way down the long corridor of the estate. She'd grown up here, living in a privileged household. At least until her father's passing. Now it was her job to take care of her sisters, and there just wasn't enough money to go around.

"Then you must have missed the part about the esteemed and handsome Claude La Cour hired personally to investigate the murderers. All the way from Paris." Mazie waggled her eyebrows.

With a huff, Clara snatched *The Star* back from her sister and flipped the paper over to read the rest of the article. The article didn't paint the local police in a good light at all, calling them lazy and incompetent, in need of a foreign detective from Paris to solve the case for them.

Due to his high success in catching criminals, Detective La Cour was widely known, even in England. But how hard was it to catch one murderer? If they were outsourcing La Cour, then surely the police really were as incompetent as the article depicted.

"You have no idea what the man looks like," she replied, shoving the periodical back into her sister's hands. The stairs creaked as she lifted her skirts and made her way down to the main floor. There in front of the unlit hearth sat Norma reading a book, oblivious to the world around her. At the age of fourteen, her youngest sister had begun to show a womanly figure. Clara was grateful none of them had to turn to prostitution to get by like many other women she knew, and she worked hard as a nurse to make it stay that way.

"Oh, but I do," Mazie insisted. "I heard he was spotted at the train station yesterday, and I went to see for myself."

Fear climbed up her body, forming slowly over her limbs like ice in the middle of a blizzard. But then the chill dissipated with a sudden crack as hot fury thawed her out. She spun on her sister, and judging by her wince, she realized she'd spoken poorly.

"You left the house?" Anger seethed with every breath through clenched teeth. "By yourself? Mazie! There is a killer on the loose. You cannot take such risks."

"But I didn't go alone! I brought my friend Emma along. And she agrees that the detective is just as handsome as people say."

Clara closed her eyes and took a few calming breaths to appease her racing heart. Her father had done this on more than one occasion to deal with difficult patients, and she found it helped herself in similar stressful situations.

Finally calm enough, she turned on her heel toward the patient rooms while Mazie followed at her heels. "I know Emma feels herself invincible with five brothers of her own, but you are smarter than this. I do not wish to see you become a victim of *Jack the Ripper.*"

To her discredit, the name on her tongue sent a thrill shooting down her body, a desire to learn more and live in the drama, so to speak, like everyone else who found a morbid fascination with the recent terrible events.

She stamped down the strange excitement and schooled her expression as she entered the patient rooms. With nowhere else to go, not even to the nearest church with it already filled to the brim, many homeless either feigned injury, if only to find a place to lay their heads for the night, or they caught a sickness from their poor living conditions.

A rattling cough pulled her attention to a frail woman lying on the floor next to a feverish infant. All the other cots were filled, and she felt terrible about making them lie on the floor. But apparently the floor was better than the woman's previous sleeping arrangements.

Open sores lined the woman's shoulder, neck, and jaw from her "two-penny hangover." How the homeless managed to sleep slung over a rope like that baffled her. And with a baby to care for? She would not be surprised if the infant was the product of her late-night activities, as the father seemed suspiciously absent.

In hushed whispers, Mazie continued the argument with similar defiant eyes that she barely recalled witnessing from their mother. "I'm not a child, Clara. I can take care of myself."

"I'm sure those poor women also thought the same of themselves."

"It's different."

"How?" She checked the splint on a young boy of eight sitting against the wall with a faraway look in his eyes. Grief clearly plagued him, as his mind wasn't quite present. But Clara took pity on him and allowed him to stay, if just for a short time, even though he was well enough to leave her care.

"I'm not going out at night."

"I suppose I should congratulate you on your impeccable survival instincts."

Her sister huffed and crossed her arms. "You are no fun to be around. This is the reason you have no friends."

No, the reason why she had no friends was that she worked herself to the bone trying to keep her sisters off the streets. But instead of refuting her, Clara simply gave her a tight smile and adjusted the white nurse apron atop her dark blue dress beneath.

Nodding her head toward a patient lying on a cot across the room, she said in a lowered voice, "If you're so confident in yourself, why don't you go and fetch the police? This one needs to be personally escorted off the premises. He has been feigning a coma for a week now just for a place to sleep. I don't want to get involved in case things get violent."

"How do you know he's not in a coma?"

"I picked up his arm and dropped it over his face. His reflexes caught at the last moment." She tapped her dip pen on her charts and poured over them for the hundredth time. "In addition to wincing when I rubbed his sternum to check for responsiveness, I know he is faking it."

It was sad to witness the lengths one would endure to battle the harsh realities that waited for them outside the door to her hospital. She loathed to send him back out into that world, but she wanted the extra cot for someone who actually needed it.

"Fine," Mazie sighed. "I'll fetch an officer."

"Don't go by yourself."

"Yes, *Mother*."

Clara rubbed her suddenly aching temples as she watched her sister leave the house. Her siblings had been much too young to remember their mother when she'd passed, and she knew she could never truly fill that role as a parent. But they had no one else. Therefore, she tried her best.

Over the next half hour, she cooled fevers with damp cloths, administered medicine to those with rattling coughs, and even quarantined another patient with smallpox in the same room as the other.

Personally, she wanted this disease far away from her sisters. But her father had never turned away a patient, and neither would she. She made sure to be careful to prevent exposure, nonetheless.

As she returned to the main floor, *The Star* sought her attention from where it rested on top of a table in the entry room next to the other periodicals about Jack the Ripper.

She picked them up and sifted through each one, comparing the mild descriptions of each murder scene. Both were depicted as similar to an animal attack but precise, which was confirmed to be a man when the Ripper had written a letter to the authorities to confirm their suspicions.

But...who could possibly do this? And why?

A knock at the door startled her into releasing a muffled scream into her hand, and she dropped the periodicals at her feet in her fright.

Her hand flew to her racing heart. Her pulse pounded through her head. And then her body temperature dropped several degrees before little by little, the warmth returned to her frozen limbs, and her unwarranted fear slowly subsided.

A self-deprecating laugh escaped her lips at her jumpy behavior. The Ripper only seemed to strike at night, and currently, it was the middle of the afternoon. She really needed to stop feeding into the morbid excitement she often told her sisters to avoid.

The person on the other side of the door knocked again, urging the rest of her body to thaw from her previous fright.

After setting the papers back onto the table, she smoothed down her apron and once more found her poise as she crossed the room and pulled open the door.

Her jaw slackened as she first found a pair of shiny, pristine black shoes. Her gaze traveled up a long pair of legs, a black, fitted coat, and then settled on a sharp, angular face with a swoop of blond bangs escaping slicked-back hair and brushing against a tall, intimidating eyebrow.

The man held a black top hat beneath one arm, and in the other hand he held an imposing cane with a silver-plated knob at the end.

And tucked into his side with her arm through his…

Was Mazie.

The man's lips lifted in a grin almost as sharp as his outfit. "The name is Detective Claude La Cour," he said in a heavy French accent. "I hope I'm not intruding."

Chapter Two

Clara stood frozen in the doorway with a slack jaw and dumb expression as she took in what could not possibly be a real person standing before her. It wasn't just his striking appearance, but there was a presence about him that demanded attention. It was almost like if she glanced away for a single moment, the shine of his aura would dim, and she'd miss the shooting star in the sky entirely.

"Ah-ah-ah," she stuttered as she finally came back to her wits and stepped aside. "Come on in."

Though, she had no idea why he'd decided to knock rather than walk in like most people did. And with Mazie clinging to his arm like a love-stricken puppy. The girl batted her eyelashes and stared at him with doe eyes the size of the moon. Judging by the man's look of indifference…

He was accustomed to constant female attention.

"Would you like some tea?" she thought to ask after her manners caught up with her.

"Decorum demands I oblige."

Again, Clara stood frozen to the spot. But this time from uncertainty. Rather than meeting her eye, he scrutinized the room, missing no detail, his gaze lingering a little longer on the hallway leading to the hospital wing of the estate. He leaned heavily on his cane while tapping his foot, Mazie all but forgotten where she spoke excitedly to him and hung on his arm like a primate desperate for attention.

Finally, she nodded and gestured down a second hallway. "This way. Most of the estate is occupied by patients, but there are rooms set aside for family and guests only."

The prominent limp of each stride and the tap, tap, tap of his cane followed her as she led him down a hallway. She felt his intense stare on her back as they entered the private drawing room overlooking what used to be a mesmerizing garden teeming with exotic plants and flowers. Now everything was overgrown and unmanageable when the Thompson family no longer employed servants to manage the yard. Several pots and a weed-filled garden with medicinal herbs gave her a small measure of comfort of what her yard used to look like. But it was almost unrecognizable. Just like the rest of her life.

The detective took a seat beside one of the windows facing the herb garden, and she couldn't help but notice he claimed one of the armchairs rather than the sofa as if to put space between Mazie and himself.

Laughter almost escaped her when Mazie scooted her own armchair closer anyway. *Almost* because the man's presence continued to rattle her, even as she disappeared into the kitchen to prepare tea for her intimidating guest.

When she returned, she hated how the china rattled with her shaking hands as she placed a cup in front of him.

Which he didn't even touch, let alone glance at. His gaze was fixed on the yard outside the window, a disapproving expression on his face. Or, perhaps, his face always looked like that. A hard man to please, it seemed.

"I apologize for the state of the property," she said, picking up a teacup of her own. But when her hands continued to rattle, and the porcelain clinked together, she abandoned the feat entirely. "I am often so busy with nursing that I don't have time to take care of the yard. It's mostly my sisters' task."

"Then they don't do a very good job of it, do they?"

Heat flamed in her cheeks, and she clasped her hands in her lap to hide the insistent trembling. Something about this man unsettled her. She wasn't usually the cowering intimidated sort.

"Oh, come now," Mazie giggled, flirtatiously touching his arm. "I have better things to do than weed and prune an overgrown garden. Like spend time with handsome gentlemen. Tell me more about yourself."

Clara pinched the bridge of her nose and took a deep breath to prevent herself from saying anything she might regret. After years of trying to raise her sisters into respectful young women, this was the fruits of her labor?

She diverted the topic back to the situation at hand. "Is there something I can help you with, Detective?"

"You've converted your home into a hospital," he commented. "Has it always been this way?"

Shaking her head, she replied, "My father had his own practice elsewhere years ago. But I've since sold the building and now operate in our home."

He tipped his head toward her, and for what seemed like the very first time, he glanced in her direction. "I am looking for the physician in charge."

Her gaze immediately jumped to his injured leg, which earned her a scowl.

"It's not for me," he scoffed. "It's for a case I am working on. Where is he?"

"If you need assistance, I am happy to provide."

The man leaned forward and rested his elbows on his knees. Her breath faltered as his stare bore through her like searing sunlight baking desert sand. "I believe we have a grave misunderstanding, Miss Thompson. I do not seek the services of a simple nurse. I need a doctor."

Her throat dried, making speaking difficult. "My father taught me everything he knew."

"Then you are not a physician at all. I know your father has passed. Are there no other doctors present?"

"It's just me. But I am fully capable of—"

"You see? The pause for tea was a tedious waste of my time. You could have told me this at the door."

Finding patience for men like this may have permanently disrupted the health of her jaw when she found herself grinding her teeth in frustration. "Just because I can't afford tuition for medical school does not make me any less of a doctor."

"It actually does." He touched his cane to the ground and stood, brushing down his coat. "I will continue my search elsewhere. Good day, Miss."

Despite needing a cane to help him walk, he still moved with fluid grace, quickly disappearing from the room as if in a hurry to find that physician he was in desperate need for. However, she only held back a snort. He'd be back. Because unless he traveled to London, he wasn't going to find anyone better than her in Whitechapel. Not when the existing poverty made this city unappealing for those practicing.

"Oh, he's so handsome!" Mazie sighed, hands clasped to her heart.

Clara stuck up her nose. "He's rude and lacks good manners. I advise you to stay away from him lest his atrocious conduct rubs off on you."

Before Mazie could reply, the bell over the door chimed as someone opened it and stumbled inside, crying in agony.

She took a deep breath to compose herself, ignoring the ache of exhaustion pulling on her eyelids as she strode out of the drawing room and toward the front door. The doctoring never ended, and half the time, she was never paid. In coin, at least. Occasionally, she'd receive a stale piece of bread or a jar of moldy jam.

But it was better than what others earned during these hard times.

She adopted her professional mask as she moved to greet the screaming patient. However, her mask melted, and her eyes shot wide open when a pale-faced man stumbled toward her with a hand held to his bleeding neck.

With a hand on his elbow, she rushed him into the infirmary wing and set him down on a cot before pulling a curtain forward for privacy. She snatched a pile of clean white cloths from the bedside table and moved his hand from his neck.

A gasp escaped her when she found two holes pierced through his flesh, profusely bleeding as if the wound had caught a vein.

Quickly, she pressed the cloth to his wound, and he cried out as if the touch pained him.

"What happened?" she demanded.

His expression contorted in a wince, his breathing shallow. And when she placed her fingers against his wrist, she found his skin clammy and his pulse weak. "I-I-I can't remember much of what happened. I was dallying with a woman in the alleyway late last night, and I woke up this morning covered in my own blood. Wh-wh-what if it was the R-r-ripper?"

Clara lifted the bloodied rags to examine the wound once again. Judging by how much it still bled, it was a miracle he wasn't lying dead on the streets.

"I don't think this was caused by the Ripper," she answered honestly, replacing the bloodied rag with a clean one. She recalled the details in *The Star* of all three incidents thus far, and none matched two holes in the neck.

"Then what?"

"I don't know." A cruel, violent prank perhaps. But it was no murderer. Most likely.

"Do you know what happened to the woman? Could she have done this to you?"

The man shook his head, but the movement caused him to sway where he sat. Dizziness must have overcome him, as he melted onto the cot and squeezed his eyes shut. "She was a small, pretty thing. Called herself Lady Stride."

Stride…

Shock coursed through her body, her patient momentarily forgotten as she jumped to her feet and rushed to grab *The Star* still lying on the table near the doorway. Her gaze quickly scanned the first of the three periodicals. When it didn't hold the information she searched for, she tossed it down in favor of the next. Still nothing.

And then she glanced over the third, her gaze stopping suddenly on the name of the latest victim, Elizabeth Stride. Could she be one of the same?

"What did you say your name was again?" she murmured half to herself.

But when she returned to the infirmary to ask the man, he was passed out cold, his face paler than ever before. She checked his pulse and pressed her ear to her monaural stethoscope to listen to his lungs. He was still alive.

However, he'd lost a lot of blood. If he were to survive, he needed care and rest.

She placed a folded, square cloth against his neck and gently wrapped another cloth around to hold it in place. Because she couldn't apply too much pressure to the wound without blocking his airway, she wasn't certain he would recover.

But she would try to save him, nonetheless.

Just as soon as she finished cleaning the dried blood from the man's skin, a woman walked in supporting what looked to be her ten-year-old daughter, a wadded cloth pressed to her arm. Likely something needing stitches.

Over the next several hours, she worked tirelessly suturing wounds, splinting bones, and administering medicine to the sick. Her younger sister, Norma, helped where she could. Despite a lack of love for the profession, Norma offered aid without complaint.

All while Mazie was out with friends doing who knew what? When Clara had been eighteen, she'd spent every waking moment at her father's side learning the craft. At eighteen, Mazie had no sense of direction. Nor did she seem to care.

Clara muttered grumpily to herself as she cleaned her workspace as the sun descended behind the city, and darkness became an unwelcome companion filled with anticipation and dread. Would any of her patients pass in the night? Would someone barge in demanding medical attention when all she wanted was to sleep for more than a few hours at a time? Would another patient sneak around the house, trying to find something to steal?

It wouldn't be the first time and certainly not the last. Each of them slept with their doors locked in three places and with a weapon beneath their pillows just in case. But she made sure to keep their own side of the house locked to prevent wandering if possible.

After checking on all her overnight patients, she stood in the foyer with a lantern held in her hand. The flickering candlelight illuminated a still and quiet house aside from the occasional hacking cough and creaking cot.

No one called out in pain. No one demanded her attention. All was quiet.

For a long moment, she gazed out the window into the darkness. City lamps drew her attention to the world outside, away from what had felt like her prison for years. Very rarely did she leave the house. Because when she left, people died. Not only that, but she and her sisters relied on the money she made doing physician's work.

Despite her longing to leave, to step into the world outside the hospital, she was stuck. Just like her father had been stuck and engrossed in his work until the day he'd died.

Shaking herself out of the past before she allowed it to consume her, she climbed the stairs to her room and slid all three locks into place.

She turned around.

And froze.

Darkness permeated the atmosphere from the open window. A light breeze brushed against the filmy curtains cascading toward the wooden floors like silky water. But what truly caught her attention...

Three gouge marks lay on either side of the sill as if an animal had dug its claws into the wood and dragged them along the frame.

Her gaze darted toward the wall nearest the window, and she spotted another three gouge marks in the leafy green wallpaper. Something or someone had been in here recently.

"Is anyone there?" she called out. Her shaking hands caused the candle flame to cast dancing shadows across the room, creating what seemed like dozens of monsters clawing their way through the dark corners.

She crossed the room and threw open her armoire. Nothing.

Next, she searched the closet, under her bed, and inspected the outside of the window for any sign of whoever had done this. She didn't quite know how, but she needed to protect her sisters from…from…whatever this was. It had been in their house, which meant she needed to search the premises for more gouge marks.

Even if her heart trembled at the thought.

She nearly turned away from the window when she discovered something small and sharp sticking out of the corner of the sill, lodged between two pieces of wood. Pinching her fingers over the object, she wiggled it free and inspected it close to her face.

Small. Black. Pointed. With the faintest curve… And impeccably strong, as it didn't break when she tried to bend it.

It was a claw. Or a fingernail. Or perhaps something in between. But she was certain this was what had caused the gouge marks.

"Ah!" She hissed through her teeth when the tip of the claw pierced her finger. Moments later, a screech echoed somewhere below, sending her heart leaping to her throat in fright.

She rushed to close the window, twisting the locks into place and sliding the curtains together before pulling her robe tighter over herself. Something had been in here. Or perhaps *someone*.

And by the look of it… She wasn't even sure it was human.

Chapter Three

He arrived promptly at noon the following day, just as she'd expected. And unfortunately, he blew through the door with his long limbs, fancy cane, and just as much attitude as the day prior.

"You have a witness," Detective Claude La Cour said in an accusatory tone. He limped after her as she fitted the newly vacant cots in the infirmary room with new sheets. After much screaming, kicking, and begging, the patient faking a coma had been dragged out of the infirmary by two officers. Clearly, he hadn't been in a coma at all unless he'd *miraculously* woken right as the police had arrived to escort him off the premises.

She grunted with the effort of lifting the mattress to fold the edge of the sheets beneath before briefly turning to answer the impatient blond detective. "How did you learn of it so quickly? I've only spoken to—" An exasperated exhale escaped her as she shook her head. Of course, Mazie had told the detective about the possible witness to Elizabeth Stride's murder.

"Where is he?" the man demanded. "Show me the patient."

"Due to patient confidentiality—"

Detective La Cour backed her against the wall in a blindingly fast motion and slapped his hand directly above her head, trapping her against his body. She gasped, her heart beating quickly at the sudden motion and when his intense blue eyes seemed to pierce directly through her soul.

She squirmed under his scrutiny, but her limbs quickly locked beneath the ice in his eyes.

"Please move aside." Surprisingly, her voice didn't quaver.

"You are impeding on official police business," he growled in his smooth French accent. "I demand that you acquiesce and show me to the man."

Defiance glared back at him as she challenged him with her own stare. Who was this man who thought he could barge into her infirmary and demand whatever he wanted? All without a single ounce of decorum in his entire body.

"Would it hurt for you to ask nicely?"

La Cour huffed as he pushed himself off the wall and crossed his arms with his cane dangling from the ends of his fingers. Like their first meeting, he made an imposing sight full of long limbs, sharp angles, and deathly glares. He brushed the swoop of his hair out of his face, but it fell right back over his eye.

"Take me to the patient. *Please.*"

She supposed she would receive no better from him and, therefore, stepped past and led him to the opposite end of the infirmary. From there, she drew back a curtain to reveal the man in question with skin as pale as death and shallow breaths moving in and out of purple lips.

"You will get no testimony from him," she explained as she once more took the man's vitals to find his pulse slow and his lungs struggling for air. "Hasn't woken since he stumbled in here yesterday. I'm not sure what happened to him, but he's not in good shape."

"Obviously." The detective leaned closer and studied the man with a careful eye. "He told you he was with Stride the night of her murder? Did he say anything else?" He tapped a long finger to his chin. "I wonder if we've found our murderer at last."

Yet, doubt clouded his voice as if he didn't believe it in the slightest.

His fingers moved toward the bandage around the man's neck. "Let me see the wound. If it's similar to the others..."

"You can't barge in here, rudely demand information, and undress what I've so painstakingly wrapped all for the sake of—" Her words cut off as the detective gasped after peeling back the bandage to reveal the double puncture wounds. Thankfully, they had stopped bleeding. But it had already done enough damage. The poor man might not live to see the next sunrise.

La Cour released a string of expletives unfit for a woman of good breeding to hear. But as it was, she'd heard more than her fair share of curse words, plus some, that it hardly fazed her. Especially when she'd used a few of them herself.

"You've missed your calling as a sailor, Detective," she said with a straight face, but a small bit of her teasing tone must have leaked through enough for him to lift his head.

"My apologies. But this wound... It's...it's..."

"Yes?"

Rather than explaining himself, he rummaged through the pockets of his coat and pulled out a yellow tape measure often utilized by seamstresses. He used it to measure the height of the man, though at this point, he should have just asked. She had all the information written down on the patient's chart.

Next, he measured the length to the wound, the angle, and jotted it down on his own small, leather-binding notebook filled with neat, elegant writing that already appeared stretched for space.

She peered over his shoulder to try to catch a glimpse of his findings, but he quickly snapped the book shut.

"Not for your eyes," he warned.

A scowl pulled on her lips as she planted her hands on her hips. "Not for my eyes? And what about *my* charts? *My* patients? Detective or not, they are not meant for your eyes, either—"

"I have horrifying details of the victims of recent murders." He tucked his notebook back into his pocket. "They are not for your eyes because the details are rather gruesome. But..." He glanced around the infirmary, his gaze lingering a little longer on a man lying on a cot with his amputated arm bound tightly with wrappings. He'd badly injured his arm in a factory accident when his wedding band had snagged on machinery and sucked the rest of his arm inside. "I suspect you could handle them."

Yes, that she could. She'd seen more than her fair share of blood and misery. It had stopped bothering her in her teenage years, and now she was indifferent to it all.

A groan from the opposite end of the infirmary pulled her attention to the woman battling an infection from childbirth. The father had taken the boy and had left the woman to recover alone. However, she hadn't recovered, and Clara feared she never would.

She measured and poured a dose of honey-scented medicine into a small vial before lifting the woman into a sitting position to help her drink. The woman cried out at the pain of simply sitting, and once administered the medicine, she slumped exhausted on the cot and closed her eyes. Perhaps at this point medicine was no longer effective. What she needed was pain relief until the infection took her.

"Does no one help you here?" the detective asked, glancing around them.

As she administered medicine to another patient, she answered, "My youngest sister, Norma, washes and folds the linens. She also handles much of the paperwork and discharging patients." She placed a thermometer into a feverish mother's mouth and next checked the temperature of her baby lying next to her. The fevers were too high, but she was confident they would pull through.

Dipping clean cloth into a bowl of cool water, she wrung them out and placed them against either forehead. It wasn't much, but it would help.

"And the middle sister?" he asked. "What does she do?"

Clara couldn't help but snort in amusement as she pinned him with a pointed stare. "It was only a matter of time before you asked about her."

"Oh? And why is that?" He leaned forward on his cane, pinning her with an equally haughty stare.

"She's the *beautiful one.*" She rolled her eyes, thinking of all the attention her sister received. It irked her. Not because it didn't happen to her but because Mazie's admirers often visited her hospital for "emergency care" if only to catch a glimpse of the beautiful blonde sister. "I don't blame you for your interest, but I ask you to take it elsewhere."

"Interest?" His expression contorted into something resembling a mix of appall and disbelief. "She is at least ten years younger than me. No interest exists, I assure you. I was simply curious about her duties."

She picked up a few piles of discarded bandages and placed them in the wash bin. "She is supposed to handle supplies and deliveries, but I can't get her to do anything half the time. She likes to pretend we still live a life of luxury and enjoys being idle. But it's fine. Because she's *beautiful.*"

Envious of her sister? Not at all. But she often wished she'd inherited her mother's blond hair rather than her father's golden copper strands.

Trying to distract her frustrated thoughts, she jotted her recent values on the existing charts and silently prayed to not receive another patient today. Maybe tomorrow. But not today. Not after the terrifying ordeal last night. Only her bedroom had received gouge marks while the rest of the house was gouge-free. Perhaps a bear had entered her window and had left promptly after. What else could it have been?

Detective La Cour cleared his throat. "I have," he cleared his throat again, "questions. About my case. Can I spare you for a few minutes?"

Clara grinned as she briefly glanced up from her charts to find him flexing his fingers over the knob of his cane and looking anywhere but at her. "I see you've discovered that I'm the only *doctor* available until you reach London. No one in the profession wants to work in Whitechapel. Not when the pay is horrendous."

"Ah. Yes. Well." Once again, he cleared his throat. "I think I will take that tea now."

"Just so you can watch it grow cold with a sneer on your face?"

He returned her grin with one of his own. "Yes. Exactly that."

She released a dramatic sigh. "Decorum demands it, I suppose."

The chuckle from his mouth caused her stomach to flutter unexpectedly, and she quickly smashed a brick over the rising emotion until it resembled a smooshed insect splattered over hot cobblestone. She refused to resemble one of those foolish, giggling girls swooning right and left over the man.

Without further ado, she prepared tea a second time for the detective. They took a seat across from each other in the drawing room with a small round table between them. This time as she placed the teacups on the table, she watched as he dropped in several cubes of sugar, stirred for a length of time, and took a sip before stirring in another cube.

It seemed the belovedly rude detective had a sweet tooth.

He rested an ankle on his opposite knee and leaned back in his chair, fixing her with another intense stare. "How much do you know about vampires, Miss Thompson?"

She laughed and shook her head. "Is this the part where I tell you to stop wasting my time and show you the door? I have work to do, Detective. I don't have time to entertain fables."

But as he continued to stare without a word, her smile fell, and discomfort twisted her belly until she thought she might retch. Had the words come from any other mouth, she might have laughed again. Unfortunately, this was Claude La Cour. Serious as could be.

"Vampires are fables," she tried again. "Made-up creatures to scare children into behaving. Nothing more."

With a shake of his head, he replied, "Vampires are very real. They are one of the creatures I hunt for a living. My department tries to cover up their existence to keep the masses from chaotic panic. I'm only telling you this now because of what you have witnessed as a...*physician.*" He nearly spit the word out as if it tasted like dirt.

Silence permeated the air like a suffocating whisper as she tried to figure out his sick little game. For what purpose was he trying to frighten her? "You are jesting."

"Stand up, if you will. I'd like to explain."

She paused as she cast him a distrustful stare. First, he had written her off entirely. And now he was spouting nonsense about vampires? Was the man a bit batty in the head?

"Hurry it up," he urged. But when she remained in her seat, he pushed himself to his feet first before holding out a hand.

She huffed and stood on her own, refusing to take the man's hand. She didn't need his help. With anything. And certainly not with standing.

The slight seemed immediately forgotten as he dropped his hand and rounded the table toward her. A part of her wanted to back away when she worried his battiness might be contagious. But she stood her ground and refused to be cowed.

"I know you have not seen wounds like your patient's before," he began. "That was clear by your expression when you first showed the man to me. They are fang marks. Created by a vampire."

Crossing her arms, she peered around him with the intention of making a timely exit. Enough of her time had been wasted for one afternoon.

"Give me a chance to explain." He leaned to the left to block her view of the exit with his body. "And if you think I'm a raving lunatic, then fine. I still have questions about my case."

"Fine." She dropped her arms to her sides and peered up at him. Her stomach dipped again when she realized just how tall he was when he stood at his full height rather than hunched over his cane.

But then she frowned. She needed to have a few words with her stomach. The detective was possibly insane. And rude. It didn't matter how handsome his face might be.

Immediately, her stomach fluttered again, and this time her heart followed as he stepped closer and loomed over her with his intimidating height. "Your patient is only a bit taller than you, and my height is wrong for the demonstration. But it will suffice." He took either arm and turned her around so her back faced him. "The position of the wound on the man's neck indicates he was attacked from behind by someone taller than him. Another man. The angle of the fang piercings show he was twelve centimeters taller. About..." He stooped lower. "Here." And then his hand hovered over her waist. "Permission to touch you?"

When her voice refused to work when the heat from his body seeped into her with its proximity, she simply nodded.

One of his hands rested on her waist, and with the other, he brushed wisps of hair away from her neck. "The vampire moved quickly. There were no other signs of fang scratches or claw marks to indicate the victim found the time to fight back. He was taken by surprise."

And then he moved closer until his breath caressed her neck, sending gooseflesh crawling across her skin.

He spoke again with hardly a whisper. "There is a scuff mark on his cheek. He must have been pushed against an alley wall, trapped as the vampire fed on him."

"There are no such things as vampires."

"Then what other reason do you offer to explain the man's wounds?"

Yes, the wounds were curious, indeed. Like nothing she'd ever seen. The perfect size for incisors. And the detective's statement made sense. But she wasn't about to believe creatures of fables were real.

"I think you are a mad, raving lunatic. That's my reasoning."

Before he had a chance to counter her words, light footsteps entered the room behind her, followed by a gasp and something heavy falling to the floor. Clara pushed Detective La Cour away and spun around to find Mazie's gaze darting between them, her eyes filled with hurt, betrayal, and anger.

"I-i-it's not what it looks like!" Clara stuttered. She cut the detective a scathing glare. Now she would have to deal with her younger sister and her delicate feelings all because of an infuriating demonstration.

Mazie sniffed and stuck up her nose. "I am able to see exactly what it is with my own eyes. If you need me, I'll be out with my friends."

Clara released a long breath of frustration as her sister turned on her heel and threw open the front door. "Don't forget to pick up the delivery on your way back! I need those medicines tonight."

And then the door slammed shut with a resounding bang.

All at once, the entire infirmary seemed to come alive when a baby wailed, a man cried out for help, and a woman screamed. Others begged for a doctor, their voices emanating from the infirmary wing.

Clara thought of nothing but her patients as she rushed down the hallway, into the infirmary, and first tended to the wailing infant. She picked up the child in her arms and bounced him gently while watching the mercury in the thermometer rise to match his temperature.

Still too high.

With the baby tucked in one arm, she dug into her cabinet of medicine, only to frown. Meadowsweet would bring down the fever, but she was all out. It was supposed to be in the delivery Mazie was to pick up today. Without a way to bring down the fevers, both the baby and the mother could die when they might otherwise make a full recovery.

"Don't you worry," she murmured as she placed a cool, damp cloth over the infant's forehead. He whipped his head from side to side until the crying grew loud enough to drown out all other begging voices in the infirmary. Thankfully, Norma helped tend to the patients as Clara minded the child. She propped him up against several pillows and popped the mouthpiece of a bottle into his mouth. Milk from the glass bottle traveled up the short tube and through the mouthpiece, into his mouth as he sucked ravenously. It was only a temporary relief from his pain, but she could do little more without that medicine.

She checked on wounds, administered laudanum and opium from what was left of her stash, and offered food and water to those recovering from their infirmities. Only when she glanced over her shoulder did she notice the detective trailing her with his gaze.

She pulled off her apron and replaced it with another with the intention of seeing to her smallpox patients upstairs, and only then did La Cour follow with his long, limping stride.

"Did your patient say anything else?" he asked, bringing the attention back to his case. "Mazie mentioned he was with Stride before she was murdered."

"If you are inquiring about Jack the Ripper, I'm afraid I don't think my patient saw the man in question. Unless these so-called *vampires* are your Ripper."

But the detective shook his head. "I'm not sure these cases are related. But I do, unfortunately, believe that Whitechapel is attracting creatures of the night."

She glanced over her shoulder on her way up the staircase and gave him a look of disgust. "Prostitutes, you mean?"

"No." He rolled his eyes. "Actual creatures of darkness. Vampires. Demons. Ghosts."

That sealed it. Detective La Cour was a nutter. But this wasn't the correct institution in which to admit him.

They needed to steer this conversation elsewhere. She'd had enough talk of vampires for her lifetime. "Why did you come the other day? Did you end up finding a doctor for your issue?"

"It wasn't *my* issue," he huffed. "Elizabeth Stride was found missing a kidney. I need a doctor to examine the body. I am unsure if you will know what you are looking at—"

"Excuse me?" She stopped directly in front of the door leading into the quarantine room and turned to face him. "I have seen the insides and outsides of more dead bodies than you will encounter in your lifetime. I'm quite certain I can identify whatever it is you are searching for."

Sure, she needed to distance herself from this lunatic, but when her pride was at stake, she couldn't help but rise to the challenge.

"Tomorrow at the morgue then," he replied with a challenging eyebrow.

"Fine."

"Fine." He placed his hat on top of his head and tipped it in her direction. "Have a good night."

A shudder raked down her spine as she watched him leave, his words reminding her of the gouge marks in her window. The claw-like item she'd found seemed to weigh heavily in the pocket of her dress, a despairing reminder of the hours she still had to pass during the night.

She almost called the detective back to show him the claw. Almost. But then she decided it would only give him the opportunity to make up a wild story about some dark creature of the night while he wore a serious expression on his face.

No... Better to keep it to herself. For now.

"It's nothing," she reassured herself. But the weight of the claw continued to burn a reminder through her pocket as she passed the next several hours taking care of her patients, all while continuously listening for the front door to open and anticipating Mazie's arrival.

Where was she? Clara needed that medicine. And fast.

But as the afternoon transitioned to dusk, and dusk settled into the dark hush of night, her annoyance slowly melted into worry. Where was she? Could someone have attacked her on the street? Was she hurt? Injured? She didn't usually stay out late unless she informed Clara first.

Not too long after, her patient—the mother of the sick baby—passed, which left the child an orphan for all she knew. No father was listed on the patient's chart, and she had no idea how to begin searching for him.

Clara braced herself against an armchair and released a worn, ragged breath. Yes, she lost patients occasionally, but it always created a pit of despair raging within her chest. A feeling of regret and incompetence encompassed her, and she couldn't stop the doubt from clouding her judgment. This could have been avoided. She could have prevented the woman's death if she'd had that medicine, if she'd had more ice, if she'd done something differently. Those two had had no one else. Only Clara.

And she'd failed them.

Her hands fisted against the armchair when her frustration won over her worry. The death could have been prevented with that medicine. It should only have taken Mazie less than an hour to fetch the delivery. Where was she?

As if on cue, the front door opened. Clara rushed down the hallway to find Mazie slipping inside.

With no delivery in her arms.

"Where have you been?" Clara hissed. "You should have been back hours ago."

Mazie slipped her gloves off and stuck up her nose. "With friends." But the stench of alcohol and tobacco indicated a merrier time than simply shopping or seeing the sights.

"Where is the package I asked you to pick up?"

Her sister turned a cold shoulder to her, hardly acknowledging her presence. "I'll get it tomorrow."

Clara's hands shook with frustration and anger as she steepled them together and pressed them to the bridge of her nose, taking a deep breath to calm herself before she replied.

"A mother died, leaving the baby an orphan and preventing us from getting paid for our efforts. And do you know what could have saved her life? Medicine to bring down the fever. Tell me, Mazie, why you neglected the one task that I asked you to complete?"

At least she had the decency to look horrified at the statement. "I-I-I didn't know anyone would die."

"No, you didn't. Because you weren't thinking about anyone but yourself." She dropped her hands to her sides as she realized this retaliation was because of her suggestive position in the drawing room with the detective. "Is this behavior because of La Cour? All of this because of a man?"

"But it's not fair!" she shouted. "I had him first."

Mazie's response alone was indication enough of her immaturity. But had Clara enabled her behavior? She, herself, had been forced to grow up quickly as a child, and her interest in her father's profession had occupied her time with scalpels, medicine, and sick patients rather than men and courtship.

In a calm manner, she replied, "I provide for all three of us. My work allows us to keep the house rather than living on the edge of poverty like many others. All I ask of you is that you help weed the garden and pick up my deliveries. But if you'd like, I can relieve you of your duties." She paused and lifted an eyebrow. "And you can find your own job to support yourself."

Mazie had the audacity to stomp her foot. "That's not fair!"

"Isn't it? I am not your mother, Mazie. I am your sister. And we all need to pull our weight around here."

Her sister threw up her arms and paced across the anteroom. "I wanted to get away from this place! Claude is from Paris. He could have taken me away from here. Given me a good life out of this hovel of a city. And you ruined it."

"I did nothing of the sort."

"Didn't you?" Tears now streamed down Mazie's face, the skin around her eyes bright red with errant emotion. "I've visited him several times. He even came to see me once. And the only thing he talks about? You. He asks questions about *you*. About his *case*. He has no interest in me. In my life."

"Then bat your eyelashes harder!"

Silence descended upon the estate like hungry wolves as Mazie's eyes flashed with shock, hurt, and betrayal. Perhaps Clara should have taken back her words, but anger and frustration continued to vex her until it became all-consuming.

If escaping Whitechapel was what her sister wanted, all it took was a few carefully placed words, a little flirting, and flaunting that natural beauty of hers. But she'd decided to acquire a difficult target—a man who was married to his job. It was not Clara's fault that all her flirting and batting eyelashes had failed.

Mazie spun on her heel, rushed up the staircase in a flurry of skirts and hair falling out of its pins, and moments later, her bedroom door slammed and echoed throughout the house.

Norma peeked over the railing, the guilt in her expression giving away the fact that she'd overheard the entire conversation. She wouldn't be surprised if the patients had overheard the shouting as well.

"What will you do?" her little sister squeaked. "That baby will follow soon without that medicine."

"Likely before sunrise," she murmured in agreement.

The window drew her attention. More specifically, to the dark blue, yellow, and pink of dusk waiting just behind. If she hurried, she might be able to reach the post office before sundown. But unfortunately, it would leave her vulnerable to travel the night alone on the way back.

With a murderer on the loose.

More specifically, a murderer of women who walked the streets alone. She was a prime target for Jack the Ripper.

But she had no choice.

And she had no time to spare.

She rushed upstairs to her room, changed into men's trousers and shirt, and tucked all her long, copper hair into a cap. Although she still looked far more feminine than a boy, she hoped the clothing was enough to deter any unwanted attention.

Without giving fear time to incubate, she stepped out of her home...

...and braved the darkness.

Chapter Four

Clara reached the post office when the lamplighter lit the first lamppost for the evening. The flicker of flame encouraged dread rather than safety as she watched the last of the sunset descend upon the horizon, leaving room for a dark chill to grab a hold of her chest and squeeze.

"Everything is fine," she murmured to herself as her soft footsteps echoed against either side of the alleyway leading to the back of the post office. The Ripper seemed to murder a new victim a week to a month after the last. The previous victim had been killed only a few days ago. Nothing would happen to Clara. Nothing at all.

Still, she glanced over her shoulder to find the alley empty and the streets quiet. Uneasiness climbed her trousers and settled in her heart from the silence. Whitechapel was never this quiet.

But...

That was *before* the murders.

By the time she reached the back door, she was breathless. But it wasn't due to physical exertion as much as fear for her own safety. She tried to twist the doorknob. Locked. And then she rapped on the door, glancing over her shoulder once more only to find darkness.

Thankfully, footsteps on the other side alerted her to someone's presence, and she quickly pulled the cap off her head to let her hair tumble freely down her back. The lock clicked followed by the rattle of a chain. And then the door swung open to reveal a thin man with a bushy mustache that contained more hairs than the top of his head.

The man held up a lantern to illuminate the dark shadows around his eyes and the permanent frown pulling on his wrinkles. "We're closed, Miss Thompson. Come back on the morrow."

"Please," she begged. When the door started to close in her face, she stuck her foot in the door to stop it from closing entirely. Pain ricocheted up her leg. Tears stung her eyes. But she tried to remain calm and collected. "I need that medicine. My sister forgot to pick it up earlier today."

Mmmhmm. *Forgot.* On purpose.

The man released a long sigh and rubbed a hand down his weary face. "Just because you ain't doin' the devil's work like everybody else." He disappeared but left the door slightly ajar. A minute later, he returned with a sealed crate and handed it to her across the threshold of the shop, exchanging it for five pence. She loathed to hand over the coin, but it was a necessary expense for her practice.

"Thank y—"

He slammed the door in her face.

Well, at least he'd given her the package rather than forcing her to return in the morning. It was a small blessing.

She tucked her hair back in her cap and clutched the crate close to her chest. It was no weapon, and the weight and size of it made it awkward to carry, but it still made her feel safer than carrying nothing at all.

Again, the silence of the city sent an eerie chill chasing each of her footsteps through the back alley. It was like venturing outside after a raging snowstorm and listening to the accompanying nothingness. Except this quiet was far from peaceful. It was like the silence that alerted the critters in a forest of a nearby predator.

Or…it might all be in her head.

"Fifteen minutes until I reach home," she quietly reassured herself. For a moment, she wasn't sure whether to talk to herself to keep herself calm or to remain quiet to prevent discovery. In the end, she decided to travel without speaking and attempted to muffle her footsteps by walking on her tiptoes.

However, the farther she traveled, the quieter the city seemed to fall. A chill seeped up from the ground and clung onto her extremities. Frosty breaths escaped each labored exhale. Shivers took a hold of her body and shook violently.

And then the fog rolled into the streets, slowly crawling across the ground until it obscured the way ahead.

Clara's breaths escaped as rapid, fearful huffs as she spun around to find fog enclosing her in the alleyway with not even a single lamppost to illuminate the way ahead. One street blended into another until she lost track of the path leading home.

Keep calm, her father had once said during a surgery to remove a patient's appendix. *One of the worst things for a doctor to have is shaky hands. No matter the outcome, you must control your fear.*

She focused on breathing slowly through her nose instead of giving into the fear pounding its fists against the inside of her ribcage. She needed to find a way home. And quickly. Not a single moment wasted on indecision and panic.

Setting the crate of supplies on the ground, she gingerly climbed on top to give her a better view above the fog continuing to creep across the ground. Although the lamp remained out of sight, she made out the outline of the clock tower of the Co-operative Wholesale Society Building. For a moment, she swore the hands on the tower lay still and unmoving, but the distortion of the fog around her likely played into the tricks on her eyes.

She stepped off the crate and reached down to pick it up but froze when the quiet scuff of slow footsteps moved her way from behind.

Her heart leaped to her throat as she spun around to find two figures approaching through the darkness. Each wore a long, black coat with a short cape billowing around their shoulders. One wore a derby hat with his face riddled with shadows while the other wore the devilish grin of someone who had won a grand prize, his long hair tied at the back of his head.

Clara gasped and abandoned her crate entirely as she turned to run in the opposite direction. But just as she neared the end of the alley, one of the men stepped blindingly fast in her path, and she crashed into his chest.

He grinned, showing off two pearly white fangs that seemed to glow like moonlight in the darkness.

"Where you goin', sweetheart?" he asked in a voice closer to a sultry purr than a foreboding hiss. "We only want to play."

She should have run. She should have wrenched herself away. But all she managed to do was stare wide-eyed at the fangs impossibly long and sharp protruding from the man's gums.

A vampire.

But it was impossible!

Before she had a chance to react, the man shoved her by the shoulders. She stumbled backward, tripped over a broken brick dislodged from the wall, and crashed into the man behind her. His chilling laughter planted a seed of dread deep within her gut, letting nothing sprout but shadows and darkness.

"Let me go!" she cried when she finally came back to her senses and elbowed her captor in the gut.

He grunted, but his impossibly strong grip only tightened further on her arms. No matter how hard she struggled against him, breaking free proved next to impossible. The vampire was strong. But it was an abnormal strength as if he were made of stone rather than flesh.

Rather than heeding her plea, the man tugged off her cap and threw it to the ground. Her hair escaped its confinement and rushed down her back. "What have we here?"

The vampire with the hat laughed and moved forward with alarming speed and grace. In only a single blink, he once more stood before her and showed off his fangs beneath a predatory grin. "I told you *he* was actually a *she*." In a sing-song voice, he said, "Feed on the men, infect the women."

He pulled out a clear vial filled with a liquid that appeared suspiciously like blood. Except it was black rather than red as a human's might be.

"We'll let you go," he cooed. "Just as soon as you drink this."

The man behind her pinned her arms to her sides. She kicked and struggled, but as if held by a giant snake, the more she struggled, the more she fell victim to his impossible strength.

In a terrifyingly alluring tone, the man with the hat leaned closer and whispered near her ear, "Don't you worry 'bout a thing, darlin'. You won't remember any of this."

Clara lifted both her legs and kicked him in the stomach, surprised when she landed the hit hard enough for him to stumble backward. But just as quickly, he rushed back to her side in a blink of movement, took a hold of her chin, and gripped hard enough to keep her from moving her head.

"What do you want?" she tried to bargain, but her words were muffled when only part of her mouth moved enough to speak. "I don't have much, but I'm sure we can come to some arrangement."

She once more stared at the fangs bared, menacing and destructive and predatory.

However, her captors only laughed. The man in the hat moved closer.

And then she screamed as loud as her lungs allowed, desperately hoping someone nearby might hear and come running to the rescue. She screamed until her voice became hoarse, until her lungs ran out of air. Until her pleas became waning embers in a blazing fire of desperation. No one was coming.

Alarm replaced her sliver of hope when the vampires only grinned at each other as if they found the sound of her screams amusing rather than threatening.

"Ah, my favorite part of this game," the man holding her said before he inhaled a deep breath of her hair and released it. "Such tasty fear."

"Focus!" the man with the vial hissed, glancing over his shoulder. "We're not the only ones out tonight."

In a quick movement, the vampire unstopped the vial and wrenched open her mouth. No amount of attempting to keep it closed did any good when he proved much stronger than she.

"Ngh!" she shouted, her words unintelligible as she tried to kick and struggle again, but the man pinning her limbs down was relentless. "Ngh lihn gneah!"

"Bottoms up," the vampire murmured and placed the vial to her lips.

But before the liquid within touched her tongue, something dark and large flew over her head in a single bound and tackled the vampire to the ground. The vial shattered against the cobblestone, spilling the dark liquid across the alleyway. Growls and hisses lifted into the air, and the vampire holding her steady swore before tossing her to the side.

She crashed into a brick wall, her cheek scraping against the rough surface.

Heavy breaths heaved in and out of her lungs as she spun around in a desperate search for an exit, for a way to escape. But then her gaze settled on the large beast attacking the first vampire with sharp black claws extending from his dark gray fingers. His form appeared mostly human but with black ridges protruding from his back and elbows. The last thing she noticed was the tail whipping out from behind him and stabbing the second vampire with its sharp end.

Deciding not to linger a second longer, she scrambled away from the fight, but her movements were slow and sloppy when terror weighed heavily on her limbs. She only managed to sprint several paces before something tackled her from behind. She wasn't sure which monster to pray that it was—the vampires or the spined creature—as both options seemed quite deadly.

She twisted sharply around and dragged her nails across the face of the long-haired vampire. He hissed in pain and flinched back, but not enough for her to free herself from beneath him.

His fangs seemed to grow longer in his mouth. His eyes flashed red. And when he moved as if to strike, she squeezed her eyes shut to brace herself for the agony that was sure to be his bite.

But at the last moment, the man's weight lifted off her as the creature tackled him to the ground and tore into him with its claws. The vampire screamed. The fog began to dissipate.

Once again, she struggled to her feet and sprinted forward but cursed when she came face to face with the dead end of the wrong side of the alleyway. She was all turned around and no longer knew which way led to the exit.

A hand clamped around her wrist. She screamed. And then the face of the vampire with the hat snarled down at her, his bleeding cheek knitting back together with each passing moment.

"This wasn't personal before," the man hissed, his eyes flashing red. "But now it is. You're coming to our den. And you're never coming back out."

A cloudy gray mist encircled them, and for the briefest moment, her entire body seemed to float as if becoming a cloud drifting along the breeze.

Her body smacked to the earth with a jarring thud. A gasping breath escaped her. She pushed herself to her hands and knees and turned her head to find the creature's long, sharp claws buried in the vampire's chest. The vampire screamed and slashed at the creature with his own sharp fingernails, but his arms weren't long enough to reach.

The creature violently tossed the vampire to the ground, pulled out a silver stake from its pocket, and thrust the sharp weapon into the man's heart.

Another scream erupted between the man's fangs, but the sound quickly cut off as his body became limp and his head rolled to the side while the color leached from his eyes until the red transitioned into a milky white in death.

The second vampire evaporated into gray mist, disappearing from the alleyway entirely as if wanting to place as much distance between himself and the creature as possible and taking the unnatural fog with him.

And then the creature turned toward her.

Her breaths quickened as she stared into its yellow eyes before her attention darted toward the claws coated in red blood. Red. Not black like whatever was in that bottle the vampires had attempted to feed her.

The creature advanced slowly with a form similar to a man's but with protruding ridges, pointed, ridged ears, and sharp teeth and claws. Its tail whipped back and forth behind him as it advanced on her with shredded clothing and no shoes on its large, monstrous feet.

Slowly, she backed up until the brick wall behind her blocked her retreat. She had been unable to escape the vampires. She would never be able to outrun whatever creature managed to kill her previous captor.

"What are you?" she whimpered. "A demon?"

The sharp cheekbones on its dark gray face became more prominent as it lifted its upper lip in a snarl. It closed the distance between them and trapped her against the wall with a clawed hand near her head.

She whimpered again, squeezing her eyes shut. In the face of death, perhaps she didn't want to know exactly when it was coming. She should never have ventured into the city by herself at night. What a foolish thing to do! There were vampires and terrifying creatures that she'd never known existed.

Until tonight.

What a foolish woman she was.

The creature moved closer and took a deep breath near her neck. She anticipated another bite, but it never came. At least not yet.

Next, it sniffed her hair, and she cracked her eyes open to find it shifting nearer still until only a breath remained between their faces.

Her heart jolted in surprise when a long, gray tongue protruded from its mouth and licked the corner of her lips, tasting her.

It leaned back and tipped its head to the side, now studying her. And surprising her once again, it spoke. No, *he* spoke. With a deep voice that could be nothing other than male. "You are not infected."

"With what? Who are you?"

Trembles took hold of her hands as she turned her head away as the only means of placing distance between them. He was no vampire, but he was another monster entirely. Perhaps one more dangerous than the last.

Finally, the creature stepped back and placed himself on the opposite side of the alley where he very nearly blended in with the shadows surrounding him. "Go," he growled, nodding his head in the direction of one end of the alleyway. "You won't receive any more trouble tonight, but you better watch yourself."

Without a moment's hesitation, Clara scrambled to snatch the crate of supplies from where she'd dropped it on the ground. She abandoned her hat entirely, not daring to give the monster time to reconsider letting her go.

She quickened her pace until she was all but sprinting in the direction of her home. Shadows seemed to close in on her. She swore fog licked at her feet. And then like a beacon in the night sky, the sight of her home filled her with hope and desperation.

She scrambled through the black gates surrounding her property, jogged up the steps to the estate, and when she finally burst inside, she slammed the door behind her, breathing heavily with her back against the wall.

Several times over, she'd almost died tonight. All for a few measly supplies. She could not allow it to happen a second time. But then again, she also couldn't allow innocent people to die on her watch. Especially not an infant.

"Did you get it?" Norma's voice startled her back to the present, smacking her back into a reality not filled with darkness, shadows, and monsters she wasn't entirely sure weren't of her own mind's making. Was she batty just like Detective La Cour?

Or had he been correct all this time? That monsters existed?

Pasting on a faux smile, she nodded her head toward the crate in her arms. "I have everything we need. Let's go save the child."

She just hoped nothing inside was broken.

Chapter Five

One didn't truly understand what they'd lost until it was gone. And yes, that meant Clara's morning coffee.

Little by little, what had been left of their stash of coffee beans in the pantry had dwindled until it was gone entirely, and she couldn't justify the expense of purchasing it any longer when she needed to choose food over alertness.

But what she wouldn't give to have it today.

For good measure, she opened the pantry for the eighth time and searched in vain for a container of coffee beans as if it might magically appear in front of her eyes.

It didn't.

And now she was going to be cranky and exhausted and running on a few hours of sleep for the rest of the day. She had to meet with the detective to examine the body, so she regrettably added shadows around her eyes to the lengthy list of what was about to make her terrible company.

She rubbed her aching, tired eyes after she finished checking on the infant. He was stable, and his fever had disappeared in the wee hours of morning. The police were scheduled to pick him up in a few hours to take him to the orphanage. There was little else Clara could do for him that those running the orphanage couldn't do themselves.

Despite the vampire mishap last night, she was grateful she'd gotten the medicine to the child in time. Even if he now had to live without a mother or father to love him and ensure his care.

Handing the child off to Norma and her patients now resting after receiving care, Clara changed from her regular blue dress and white apron to a gray long-sleeved blouse tucked into a dark gray plaid skirt. The only pop of color she allowed was a dark red belt matching the ribbon flower pinned to her bonnet.

Only at the door did she realize that the gray likely enhanced the dark shadows beneath her eyes.

The first step outside blinded her as the piercing rays of sunlight broke through the clouds overhead and offered an immediate headache. Still, she was grateful for the light. Venturing into the city with nothing other than darkness to follow in every waking footstep was not high on her to-do-again list. In fact, it made it on her to-never-do-again list entirely.

Taking a deep, exhausted breath, she exited the gates, only to freeze as clomping hooves alerted her to the carriage pulling up to the estate. Instinctively, she backed up until her shoulders brushed against the bars of the gate, and she slowly reached into her basket filled with medical supplies until her fingers grasped the scalpel hiding within.

She refused to be taken off guard by *vampires* without a good fight.

However, as the carriage rolled to a stop, Detective La Cour stepped out. Her defenses fell as a relieved sigh, and her hand dropped to her side.

"Why are you here?" she asked. "I'm supposed to meet you."

"I'm not entirely rude, Miss Thompson." His mouth twitched as if he found his statement amusing. "I'm not about to make you walk the entire way to the morgue."

"Not entirely?" She raised an eyebrow, never breaking eye contact as she stepped into the carriage as he held open the door for her. Only when he joined her, closed the door, and pounded on the top of the carriage to signal for the driver to move did she say, "So you admit you're a little bit rude then."

"I admit nothing."

The carriage lurched forward, and in her state of exhaustion, she lost her balance and braced her hand on La Cour's knee across from her. She quickly snatched it back, her eyes wide with mortification.

"I apologize."

"No harm done." He pulled out his small notebook, and she swore it looked even more battered and bruised than only yesterday.

Teacups and teacakes, had it only been yesterday? It felt like a lifetime ago.

In the dim light of the carriage, she noticed the dark shadows beneath his eyes, his rumpled hair, the wrinkled clothing. Almost as if he'd slept at his desk rather than changing into a new pair of clothes the next day.

"You look tired," she commented.

"*I* look tired? You look like you were up with patients until dawn." He chuckled and ran a hand over his face. "I didn't get much sleep last night. I was buried in paperwork and charting the case." He took a sip from a canteen, and the aroma of coffee hit her like a ton of mouthwatering bricks smashing into her senses at full force.

Unfortunately, he noticed her perk up.

"You need it more than I do." He handed his canteen over, and in her state of exhaustion, she shamelessly took a sip of the hot, bitter liquid. She sighed in relief when her mind instantly became alert, if only for the promise of the caffeine within. It was much better than tea to keep her going today, that was for certain.

With brows furrowed, the detective flipped through his notebook and rubbed a hand over his chin. For a moment, she studied the sharp angles of his face and the strand of hair flopping over his eye. Only yesterday, she'd thought him in need of an asylum.

But today?

She couldn't help but wonder just how much of his claims were true.

She cleared her throat to distract from her discomforting thoughts. "What will I be looking for at the morgue?"

He shrugged one shoulder and glanced briefly at her before returning his attention to his notebook. "I don't know. Anything. I cannot make heads or tails of the damage. The coroner is pathetically useless. Even I can tell he had no idea what he was doing after the autopsy for the second victim. I cringe to think what kind of damage he might have caused with the third."

"Surely, it can't be that bad."

This time, he set his notebook in his lap to give her a pointed look. "He sliced a lung and the heart attempting the feat. Even a drunkard off the street would be more competent than this imbecile."

Clara quickly ducked her head and covered her mouth with a hand to keep herself from laughing. Yes, the detective might be rude, but he had an amusing sense of humor.

"Ah, here we are," he murmured moments before the carriage rolled to a stop in front of the morgue. It was as if a cloud passed over the sky, sending the world spiraling into a morbid sense of darkness. A murder of crows perched in a tree above the building, likely drawn to the smell of death and decay.

The detective produced a handkerchief from his pocket with a flourish and handed it to her, also finding one for himself. "The smell isn't too bad. But better to be safe. Just in case."

She gratefully accepted it from him. "I assure you, the things I have smelled at my infirmary pale in comparison to a decomposing body."

He stopped on the step down from the carriage and studied her over his shoulder. "Huh."

"What is it?"

He shook his head, stepped to the ground, and held out a hand to help her out of the carriage. "It's nothing. Only that you continue to surprise me, Miss Thompson."

This time, she couldn't help but laugh as she accepted his strong hand, his long fingers momentarily wrapped around hers. "Is it so surprising that a young lady might have an interest in the macabre?" Well, she wasn't quite as young as she used to be and was considered a spinster to the upper-class society, but she did not feel like an old maid. Yet.

"Yes," he chuckled. "A young lady, such as yourself, should be interested in courtship and marriage, babies and sewing. Instead, your eyes light up at the very mention of human dissection."

She rolled her eyes playfully. "Which is why I'm not married. Any such husband would forbid me from practicing my craft. I won't give it up for anybody."

"And if your husband supported your craft?"

Her gaze snapped toward the detective, and suddenly she found her hands stealing the moisture directly from her mouth. It dried while perspiration only seemed to grow colder on her palms.

His expression remained blank, and his intentions entirely unreadable. Therefore, she opted for more humor. "The poor sap would be thoroughly wrapped around my little finger if that were the case. Anyway, we're here."

They reached the door of the building, and the strong scent of chemicals and decay hit her nose like a hammer to the skull. From previous experience, she knew after a few minutes, she would become desensitized to the smell. But the first few breaths were always the most difficult.

"D-d-detective," a short man with a patchy beard said as he rushed forward. But as La Cour pushed past him as if he confidently knew where he was headed, the shorter man kept up at his side like a dog obediently following its master. "The body is ready for…" He trailed off and stared at Clara as if he'd never seen a woman in his life. However, the prolonged staring became uncomfortable, even more so when his mouth dropped open and he was dumb with silence.

"Eyes ahead, Coroner," the detective barked. "We all know she's beautiful, but it's rude to stare."

At first, surprise jolted through her body at the man's words. But then a scowl pulled on her mouth, and she clutched her basket tight to her chest. Was he trying to belittle her? What was his game?

The coroner showed them the prepared body lying on a table, and Clara immediately went to work as she set out her tools on a nearby table. The short man retreated to a dark corner while La Cour remained by her side, a little too close for her liking.

The moment the silence stretched a bit too long, she murmured, "There is no need to mock me."

"Mock you?" He reeled back as if she'd struck him in the face. "Do you even realize at least half of your patients who were conscious followed you with their lovestruck gazes when you weren't watching? I assumed you knew you were a beautiful woman." He paused and pressed his lips together. "It seems you don't."

Her face burned at the blunt comment. She would have assumed he was now mocking *and* teasing her. But the sincerity in his eyes threw her off center.

"Well then." She tied an apron around her dress before turning back to the body. "It's a good thing Mazie doesn't like being near my patients. No one would give me a second glance."

He snorted but made no other comments about her appearance. Though the moment she opened the body to peer inside, she noticed he seemed just as hyperfixed on the task at hand as she was.

"Mmhmm," she murmured as she carefully examined the insides. "Missing a kidney. A slice to a lung and the heart." She lowered her voice as she briefly glanced at the coroner hiding in the corner like a scared little mouse. "The coroner, indeed, bungled the autopsy."

"If it were in my power, I'd sack him."

Turning her head to meet his eye, she jested, "If the sacking came from you, I think he'd go off trotting happily because you gave him the time of day at all."

Another snort, but this one came with a lingering grin. "I do have that effect on people."

"Clearly." She turned back to her work to study the clean slice across the woman's neck next. Something was odd about it. The slice was too large to be a knife but too clean and precise to be from an animal attack. "Hmm…"

"What is it?"

Instead of answering, she continued her examination by comparing the slice in the woman's abdomen to the one on her neck. They matched.

"This is interesting." She pointed to the end of the slit on the neck and next the abdomen. "If you see here, there is first a puncture wound a bit larger than the slice. Puncture, then slice. Almost like…" She trailed off, her eyebrows furrowing as she spotted something abnormal hiding within the stretches and folds of the woman's intestines.

"Like what?"

Again, she didn't answer as she snatched her tweezers and dug in as carefully as she dared. After a few missed attempts, she finally managed to grab onto the item with the tweezers and pulled it out of the body, holding it up to the light.

A black claw.

Identical to the one she'd found lodged into her window frame. But she wasn't about to tell him that, and she wasn't entirely sure why.

"What is this?" he murmured, taking the tweezers from her and holding the claw close to his face. "This is not human, but I've never seen anything like it."

"Not even from the creatures you supposedly hunt?"

He shook his head. "But you're correct. This is no mere animal attack. This is something...*other*."

He placed the claw on top of a handkerchief, folded it safely inside, and tucked it into his pocket.

She lifted an eyebrow. "Stealing evidence, Detective?"

The man leaned closer until the mint on his breath drowned out the other smells wafting up from the morgue. "As far as the local police are concerned, this is a knife wound. They cannot know what it really is. Panic, remember?"

"I remember."

When she found no evidence other than the claw, she started to put the body back together and sew up the autopsy incision. Without glancing his way, she asked the detective, "What, exactly, are you hunting?"

Because now she believed him. About all of it. About the vampires and the creatures that go bump in the night.

"You said *what* and not *who*."

She nodded. "If you aren't hunting a vampire, then what *are* you hunting?"

He frowned and opened his notebook somewhere near the middle where he kept a bookmark within the pages. "I don't know. I haven't encountered such a creature before. It doesn't have the same hunting patterns as a vampire."

"But the authorities don't know you're hunting a creature, do they? They think you're hunting a man."

His lips pressed into a thin line, causing his scar to become more prominent across his mouth. "The average police? No. Not at all. But those who hired me? Yes. They know that what I'm hunting is not human."

"It makes more sense why they hired outside help then. You are an actual expert in your field. Just not the one I expected."

Her gaze lingered a little longer on the scar on his mouth, and unfortunately, he noticed.

A smirk lifted on his face as he touched the place where his scar resided. "Those in my field call it my 'kiss with a demon.'"

"A real demon? They don't actually exist." But then a cold sweat broke out across her hands, and her needle nearly slipped from her fingers. "Correct?"

His smirk refused to fade. "Some say I fought against a succubus and lived. Others say the demon's kiss was as sharp as her bite."

"And the truth?"

Instead of divulging the information, he simply turned with a grin stretched across his mouth and avoided the answer altogether.

Her focus returned to tying off the last few stitches. "I was curious about what you thought of my sister," she asked hesitantly. If there was a way she could fix what Mazie accused her of doing despite its lack of truth, she wanted to try.

"Which one?" he replied distractedly.

"The older of the two. Mazie."

A frown pulled on his mouth, and he remained silent for a few moments as he scribbled notes down in his little book. "I'm not answering that."

"Why not?"

"Because no one will like the answer, and if I can avoid making you abhor me, I will."

His frown seemed to transfer to her as she cleaned and packed up her medical instruments. If Mazie wanted to escape Whitechapel, all she needed to do was bat her eyelashes and look pretty. Any wealthy man might snatch her up in a heartbeat. Unless his name was Claude La Cour—a man married to his work.

La Cour sighed and finally tucked his notebook into his pocket. "Mazie is a lovely young woman who is nearly *half my age* and sticks to my clothing like an unwanted burr. She has a place somewhere, but not with me. Does that satisfy you?"

"Blunt, a little bit rude, and to the point? Yes, it does." She placed her supplies in her basket and tucked a cloth around them. She wouldn't tell her sister what he'd said, but the matter was done. He wasn't interested, and that was that.

Prolonged silence filled the morgue as she untied her apron and folded it neatly on top of the basket. For a moment, she thought the detective had nothing else to say on the matter, but then he spoke.

"Are you going to ask what I think of *you?*"

Her head snapped up to find his intense blue eyes focused on her, almost as if he'd set his sight on an elk during a hunt and refused to look away for a single moment lest it bound away in fright.

In truth, her own legs itched to leap away, to escape this foreignly impossible situation. Especially when she wasn't quite certain what he was trying to accomplish with such a question.

"I can imagine quite well what you think of me," she said as she looped the handle of the basket around her arm. "I've heard it time and again. Poor Miss Thompson. A mother to her sisters. No marriage prospects of her own. Can't lure a man with such a disrespectful position for a woman." She huffed and turned away. "I don't want to hear it again. Not from you."

It would only cause more humiliation coming from his blunt and honest mouth.

"I don't think that." He sighed. "I know I came across that way when we first met. But I admire your dedication. I respect your commitment to your trade. And—"

She spun around and pointed a finger at his face. "What do you want, Detective? If you're attempting to butter me up, save it for someone who will fall for your charm. If you want something, then just say it."

"I wish to call on you again!" he blurted.

Her eyes widened. Slowly, her hand fell to her side in disbelief. Even the coroner slipped out of the room as if mortified on her behalf. The only time a man came to see her was when they wanted drugs or to sleep in the infirmary for the night. But to call on her? As in courtship?

"What do you really want?" she rasped. "A favor? Drugs? Another glimpse of my sister?"

He captured her hand in a movement too quick for her to pull away and cupped it between both of his. "Tea and biscuits in your drawing room?"

"With Mazie present, I presume."

He shook his head. "Just you and I."

She stared dumbfoundedly at him, trying to register his words and intentions. The handsome, hotshot paranormal detective from Paris wanted to court *her*? She didn't believe it. What was his angle?

"I-I-I should go." She tore her hand out of his grip and backed up, searching frantically for the door behind her. When she located the door handle, she turned with enough force to stumble outside.

"I'll give you a ride home."

"No! I mean, it's a nice, warm day. And I would like the exercise."

"Clara—"

The use of her given name spurred her panic faster, and she spun around and walked quickly away from him even when her legs itched to run. Surely, he was not truly sincere with his intentions toward her.

She refused for a man to humiliate her again.

Refused!

Unfortunately, her confusion and fluster followed her all the way home, and it refused to unlatch from her mind as she spent the remainder of the day with her patients. Alone. Because that was her fate. That was what *he* had said. Someone who had courted her years ago who had thought he could convince her away from her profession to become a mother and housewife. And *he* was right.

When her own self-doubt clung to her clothing like a medicine stain, she wearily climbed the stairs to the upper floor late at night while her patients slept soundly downstairs. For now. More often than not, someone woke in the dreary hours of night screaming for some reason or another. It was so common an occurrence in this household that Mazie and Norma slept right through it. But Clara? No, she could never sleep through it.

One by one, she pulled the pins out of her hair and placed them inside her apron pocket. For once, her hair wasn't a kinky mass of a mess, rather curling nicely over her shoulders and down her back. If only she got to enjoy them for longer than just a few minutes before she slept on it and made it look like a rat's nest by morning.

She opened her mouth in a large yawn as she entered her room and set her lantern down on the table beside her bed.

But then she felt the cold, chilling presence of someone else in the room moments before a draft from the open window caressed her skin. It was the way gooseflesh crawled across her arms. The way the back of her neck prickled with discomfort. The way every part of her body became alert.

She spun around and pulled out a scalpel from her pocket, holding it in both hands to protect herself from the threat. The knife may be small, but it was better than nothing.

"Who's there?" she cried, forcing herself to be brave rather than give into the wallowing fear trying to consume her whole.

Her gaze darted along the shadows flickering across the wall with each twirl and bend of the lantern flame. And then she saw him.

Chapter Six

The creature from the night of the vampire attack stood near the wall, easy to miss when he blended in with the shadows. The spikes on his back appeared more pointed and formidable than ever, and his claws almost seemed to grow longer with the flex of his fingers. The same ripped and broken rags for clothing covered his body, revealing the chiseled muscles blatantly showing beneath.

Black strands of hair fell over his face, but instead of pushing them away from his eyes, he continued to stare back at her with his yellow gaze. Almost as if wary of her. Cautious.

If he wanted to kill her, he most certainly could. After witnessing his lethal speed and prowess against the vampires, she knew one wrong move might be her last.

Despite her quavering voice, she jested, "There is a front door for a reason. It's rude to enter through a lady's window." And to make sure she knew he'd been there before, she added, "Again."

A deep, gravelly voice spoke back, "I wanted to see if you were well."

"No fang marks in my neck." She swallowed as her body chilled with fear when she glanced at the sharp, pointed claws protruding from each finger. "No claws in my chest."

"I won't hurt you."

"Then why are you here?" A part of her thought she might have been hallucinating.

At least until the monster took a step closer into the light, which further illuminated the gray of his skin, the yellow of his eyes, the sharp spines on his back and elbows.

He spoke again, his voice like the deep rumble of a large cart passing outside the window on the street. "A single drop of that blood on your lips could have infected you. I came to make sure that was not the case."

Nothing made sense anymore. Vampires? Terrifying creatures? Infectious blood? At this point, she might as well check herself into the asylum.

The...*thing*...took another step closer, further illuminating his body in the lantern light. That's when she noticed the sharp fingernail-like claws extending from each finger. Except...

Two were missing, each chipped to the nub.

And then she made the connection.

The claw lodged into her door frame. The claw buried in Elizabeth Stride's abdomen. They were the same. And unless there were multiple of him skulking about the streets...

"You are Jack the Ripper," she said breathlessly, unsure whether fascination or terror was going to cause her to faint. Because suddenly, she felt extremely light-headed. The Ripper was in her room. He had been there more than once. Perhaps he had come to finish the job from the alleyway.

Despite her frozen limbs, she managed to lean backward enough for her shoulders to brush against the farthest wall of the room. She was trapped. The Ripper had her cornered.

His tail swished back and forth with agitation, though he didn't advance. "You don't understand. No one understands. I'm not a murderer."

"Yet, it was *your* claw found in one of the victims…wasn't it?" Her hands shook some more. "Did you mean to kill her?"

This time, his tail fell limp behind him, and his shoulders slumped. "I had no choice. She was infected."

"With some sort of blood."

He ducked his head and nodded. "My blood. Those vampires? They kept me captive. Took a lot of my blood. Planned to use it to infect the people of Whitechapel."

The vampire's words returned to her mind with a stumbling crash. *Feed on the men, infect the women.*

She nearly kicked herself when her medical curiosity took over, and her fear took the corner seat in the mental carriage. "Your blood can only infect women."

His ears momentarily flattened with evident surprise. "How did you know that?"

"I'm more intelligent than I look?" she jested, fighting the urge to collapse into a chair. Or onto the ground. Whichever was closer. "What are you? Some sort of vampire?" But then her gaze raked over his chiseled muscles, and she took another guess. "A gargoyle?"

"I'm a ghoul." He pinned her with a stare. "Are you going to run off to your detective friend and tell him what I am? He's been hunting me for some time."

"I haven't said anything." She clamped her mouth shut, realizing the precarious situation she'd found herself in. No one knew what was in her room. If she screamed, she might only put her sisters and patients in danger.

Then again, she preferred that none of them find her body mutilated with her guts strewn all over her and her kidney missing in a large pool of her own blood.

"Y-y-you were here before." She hated how her voice shook, but in the face of a monster, a *ghoul*, it couldn't be helped. Especially when her hands ached and her fingers turned white from clutching the scalpel in her hands so tightly. "In my room. Why?"

"While I'm being hunted by your detective, I'm trying to rid Whitechapel of vampires. You had a patient who was bitten. I wanted to make sure he wasn't going to transition."

"Why my room?"

The corner of the monster's mouth twitched as he gestured toward the window. "There's a trellis I could climb.

It was easier than walking through the front door. I might have given someone a good startle."

On any other day, she might have laughed at the image his words conjured up. But she was closer to choking on her own fear than releasing a chuckle. "What happens if someone is infected?"

Another step closer, near enough for her to catch a glimpse of his sharp, black claws on his large feet. "They become a ghoul like me. But more...feral."

"And you want to prevent that? Why?" Aside from the obvious, of course.

He released a long breath and closed his eyes. Without the yellow of his irises, he nearly blended right into the shadows with his dark coloring. Finally, he opened them again, revealing the sadness in his expression.

"A ghoul is created, not born. I had no choice in the matter for my own transition. But I would not wish this existence on anyone else. Therefore, I kill those who are infected. There is no other option."

Slowly, she lowered her scalpel to her side. It was a foolish thing to do. But she was feeling rather foolish tonight. "Why, though?"

His attention turned toward the window and the darkness lingering outside. "Male ghouls are created. Female ghouls are turned. And the females are incredibly infectious, ravenous blood-drinkers. Half of Whitechapel would get turned like them. The other half would die horrific deaths because of their feral thirst."

"You would have killed me."

"I did my best to prevent you from getting infected."

She recalled getting cornered by vampires and nearly forced to drink the blood. The *ghoul's* blood. And then she remembered him fighting the vampires while nothing she did could do any damage against their far superior strength.

"You're sure I'm not infected?"

"Believe me, you'd know. But…"

"But?"

"There are ways to make sure."

The last thing she wanted was to scour the streets in the dead of night with a feral thirst for blood, killing, and destruction. Which was why she held perfectly still, fighting against her instincts to run in the presence of a monster, as the ghoul approached with agile movements. She could tell he was trying to move slowly, but he was too quick and graceful to manage the feat entirely.

She still jumped and gasped in a breath when he almost seemed to disappear and reappear directly in front of her. She dropped her scalpel to the floor. Her body was too petrified to retrieve it. Not a single sound escaped her despite her desire to cry out for help. But help for what? The ghoul wasn't hurting her. He wasn't threatening her. He was just…scary to look at. Inhuman. A monster.

And he was the Whitechapel Murderer.

"May I touch you?" he asked softly, though any sort of gentleness was lessened by the gravel in his voice.

"Do I have a choice?"

"Always."

For a few long moments, she stared back at him, debating between ducking beneath his arm to flee her room, and braving her fears to find out what he had planned.

Finally, she nodded and held perfectly still.

The heat of his body crossed the short distance between them as he took that last step toward her. His piercing yellow eyes penetrated her soul. His soft, gentle touch spurred her heart into an erratic, unexpected rhythm as he took her hand and brushed a thumb against her wrist.

And then surprise shook her to the core when he cradled her hand tenderly as if he were an infatuated gentleman rather than a creature she had watched tear apart two vampires with its very own claws.

"This will only hurt a little, but it will cause no lasting damage. I promise."

Before she found a chance to break free from the spell of his ensnaring gaze, she inhaled sharply when she felt the sharp prick of his claw against her wrist.

Instinctively, she tried to snatch her hand back, but he held on tightly to prevent her from retracting it entirely. But then his grip loosened as if giving her the chance to take back her permission.

She didn't.

Rather, she wanted to know the truth. Was she infected?

A small droplet of blood pooled on her wrist, a perfect circle created from the tiny pinprick of his claw.

He lifted her hand higher but then took her entirely off guard as his dark gray tongue caught the droplet from her wrist. Heat flushed through her face. Her chest. Her entire body. Until it felt as if she stood in the inferno of the blazing afternoon sun in the desert in the middle of summer. Fluster tied her tongue in a knot, preventing her from speaking anything more than a stuttering exclamation of shock.

Lastly, her heart betrayed her as it pounded against her ribcage, as her pulse thundered through her veins.

Surely, the ghoul could feel it where he held onto her hand, where his tongue licked another droplet off her wrist. And if he could somehow see in the dark, he likely wouldn't miss the blush rising to her cheeks and giving her a rosy complexion.

The claws from the hand encircling her forearm brushed lightly against her skin, sending a wave of gooseflesh crawling to her shoulders. His touch was soft. Warm. And unexpectedly thrilling.

"And?" she whispered, watching the way his tongue ran across his bottom lip to catch the remainder of her blood. "Will you kill me? Or let me go?"

"Not you. No."

She blinked several times as she realized she wasn't sure which question he'd answered, and she didn't get the chance to ask.

He said, "I hope you can convince your detective friend to stop looking for me. It will only end badly for him."

"Detective La Cour is determined."

"And that makes him foolish. Convince him to stop."

But recalling the fierce determination in his every pore, she wasn't sure anything she could say would convince him to call off his hunt for this…this…*ghoul*.

"I'll try," she promised instead.

"Good." He flipped her hand over and lifted it to his lips, kissing the back of her fingers. Another flush scorched her, and the accompanying shock seemed to nail her feet to the floor and steal any lucid thoughts directly from her mind.

The ghoul dropped her hand suddenly right before the door on the opposite side of the room slammed open and hit the wall. Mazie stormed inside and pointed a furious finger at her.

"You went and got the package?" her sister shouted, eyebrows slanted downward with anger. "That was my job, and you should have let me do it. I was capable of doing it on my own without you interfering. Therefore, I went all the way to the post office today. For what? To find out you already picked it up?"

"I needed it yesterday, Mazie," Clara replied calmly as she surreptitiously glanced over her shoulder. The ghoul lingered in the shadows, blended in with the wall well enough for Mazie's eyes to pass over him entirely. "Although the mother died, the baby survived. I had no choice."

Mazie stalked back toward the door but then spun around with her finger still pointing toward her. "You think you are better than us. You have always thought yourself better. Arrogant and condescending. I hate the way you treat me. Like my only strength is finding a husband. You think I'm stupid."

"Mazie—"

But her sister spun on her heel and stormed out of the room, leaving a guilty silence in her wake.

Clara pinched the bridge of her nose and breathed a deep sigh. She didn't know how to handle this. All she was trying to do was take care of her family and her patients. But pride and delicate feelings? She was not equipped with the knowledge to deal with this.

Remembering she had an audience, she turned around. "What did you mean when you said…" Her words trailed off when she found the room empty save for a pair of flimsy curtains billowing in the gentle breeze.

Jack the Ripper was gone. And all she had of him was the pinprick of blood on her wrist and confusing feelings swirling in her chest.

A monster had kissed her hand. And she had liked it.

She released a breathy, disbelieving chuckle and rolled her eyes. It looked as if it were time to check herself into the batty house. Because dallying with the Ripper was a one-way street to either death or an insane asylum.

Chapter Seven

They arrived at half past noon. Full and vibrant with a sweet aroma that managed to quell the stench of sickness and pain of the infirmary.

Clara stared wide-eyed at the bouquet of flowers resting within a vase on the drawing room table, the pinks, yellows, and reds a stark contrast to the white and light blue of the room around her and Norma.

She remained several steps away from the flowers, almost as if she were to touch them, she might catch a case of poison ivy and break out in hives.

"You're sure they're for me?" she breathed.

Not once in her life had she ever received flowers. The only bouquets to grace this household were the ones Mazie collected from admirers. Which were often innumerable. It was any wonder Mazie hadn't chosen a husband yet. But now Clara suspected she was holding out for someone foreign. Someone like…

Claude La Cour.

"'*For Clara,*'" Norma read. "'*A thank you for yesterday. All my adoration, Claude.*'" A sly grin pulled up on Norma's lips as she fanned her face with the small note card. "Flowers and informally using your given name? I think he's attempting to court you."

"*Attempting* is the right word here." Still, she stared slack-jawed at the bouquet, still in disbelief. She was too old for this. Too old to be swept away in the throes of courtship and passion. Too old for men searching for a young bride to give them plenty of babies and to be chained to the oven for the majority of the day.

Men didn't *give* Clara flowers. Ever. What was the detective trying to do? What did he want from her that she could possibly give?

She didn't trust him. Not for a single second. First yesterday and now today? She was beginning to grow highly suspicious of his intentions.

"Is anyone there?" a man shouted from the direction of the infirmary. "Help! Please help."

Clara spun around and rushed down the hallway and into the infirmary only to find one of her long-term patients stumbling out of one of the isolated infirmary rooms with his hand against the wall guiding him forward. His gaze was distant, confirming her fears.

He'd gone blind.

"Mr. Harvey," she said as she took his hand and squeezed. "I'm Nurse Thompson. Allow me to guide you back to your room, and I can answer any questions you might have."

Instead of following when she tugged lightly on his hand, he broke down in tears, his opposite hand covering his eyes. "Why can't I see? Why is my sight gone?"

She released a long breath and gave him a look of sympathy that he couldn't see. "You contracted scarlet fever. You were in bed for a long time. But the fever spread. It's lucky you are alive."

"But my sight is gone!"

"I'm sorry. I did everything I could to cure you. But sometimes—"

"You did this to me!" he screamed, wrenching his hand away. "You made me blind. This is your fault."

"Now, sir, please calm down, and we can discuss your options in another room—"

"I'm blind because of you! How could you do this to me?"

The patient moved so quickly, Clara found no time to dodge when he struck out with his fist. She cried out in alarm and instinctively flinched with her hands braced in front of her face. But rather than the man's fist making contact, someone caught the blow with his own hand and twisted until the patient's arm was bent precariously behind his back.

Her eyes shot wide open in shock to find Detective La Cour standing before her, protecting her from the threat.

"Now, why on God's green earth would you strike a woman?" he asked the patient in a low, threatening tone.

Something between a stutter and a pained whimper escaped Mr. Harvey's mouth. "She did this to me. It's her fault."

The detective twisted a little harder until Mr. Harvey yielded by hanging his head. "Up to thirty percent of people die after contracting scarlet fever. It's not uncommon to go blind should you survive. But do you know what's not curable? Your conscience if you strike a woman." He shoved the man forward and scowled. "You look well enough to walk on your own. I think you can find your own way home from here."

Clara could do nothing other than watch in shock as her patient stumbled away as if he had a predator on his heels. He ran into the wall a couple of times and then a door frame. But he *did* manage to leave the house on his own.

"You discharged a patient without my permission?" Clara hissed the moment La Cour turned back to her. "This is *my* infirmary. You had no right!"

His defensive scowl stared back at her as he crossed his arms over his chest. "And I should have just let him hit you? Should he have stayed, he may have tried to strike you again."

"It wouldn't have been the first time."

His eyes widened with shock. "He's done it before?"

With a shake of her head, she sighed and fixed the strand of hair that had come loose from its pins. "Unfortunately, people who work in the medical field occasionally get hit by their patients. And with the added lack of respect for a woman providing care, it has happened to me more than it had my father. It happens, Detective. That still doesn't mean you had any right to discharge my patient for me."

"I had no right?" Despite hunching over his cane, he still towered over her. But his presence wasn't threatening. Rather, it was…comforting. "I work on the police force, and right now, I am an extension of the Whitechapel authorities while I'm here. As such, I have every right to escort a threat off the premises."

They glared at one another, each silently battling for the upper hand in their argument. She refused to budge. Then again, he seemed determined to be just as stubborn as she.

"Would you like some tea?" she asked angrily.

"Yes, thank you," he replied in a curt tone.

The glare continued until she finally conceded with a huff. Infuriating man! She'd had the situation handled. Mostly.

She led him back toward the drawing room…

…but then stopped short when she found the glass vase shattered across the ground and flower stems and petals strewn about as if a gust of fierce wind had ripped through the window and destroyed the bouquet.

Her pulse slowed. Shock slowly dissipated into defeat. An ache beat hard against her chest. And no matter how hard she tried to tear her gaze away, she couldn't stop it from roaming over the crumpled petals, the broken stems, the shards of glass.

Behind her, the detective made a tsking noise with his mouth. "Hmm… It seems as if my gift was ill-received."

The first flowers she had ever been gifted from a man, and it was strewn all over the floor. For some reason, despite La Cour's intentions, the sight created a pang of disappointment in her chest, enough for her eyes to water with unexplainable grief.

Her gaze darted toward the flicker of blue moving in the corner in time to find Mazie staring at her with hatred burning in her eyes and green and yellow stains on her fingers. The sister she knew had never been cruel. But this?

This was unimaginably cruel, especially after everything she'd sacrificed for Mazie and Norma.

Clara averted her gaze moments before Mazie slipped out of the room. The detective didn't seem to notice the quick exchange, and she wanted to keep it from him as well.

To hide the tears pooling in her eyes, she knelt to the ground and gingerly picked up each mutilated stem and petal and placed it into a nearby basket.

"I-I-I must have knocked the vase over when I heard my patient scream," she said. "I'm sorry."

"There is no need to apologize, I assure you." To her shock, he also knelt beside her despite favoring one leg and helped her clean up the mess. The corner of his mouth twitched, and she braced herself for whatever wit was about to escape. "Are you positive you don't own a puppy? This mess is quite thorough."

"I'm sure," she replied with a laugh, turning her head to dab at her tears without him noticing.

"Do you like dogs?"

She shrugged, still attempting to hide her smile with a turned head. "My father always said that a dog had no place in a hospital. It would be great company, however."

More tears pricked her eyes, and she internally berated herself for her lack of composure. She was lonely. Had been for a long time. A canine companion would be nice to help quell that loneliness.

The soft press of a handkerchief in her palm startled her, and her gaze involuntarily snapped toward La Cour, but he was already on the opposite end of the table with her basket picking up shards of glass. Not once did he glance her way, almost as if giving her privacy.

Gratitude swelled within her chest as she dabbed at her eyes with his handkerchief. So much had happened in the past several weeks that it was difficult to maintain that composure she so desperately wanted. Death. Vampires. A ghoul. A sister who hated her. Almost getting struck by a patient. It was a lot to take in.

When her tears finally dried, she cleared her throat. "Did…did you ever figure out what that monster was?" she asked nonchalantly. "Jack the Ripper, I mean."

He frowned as he placed the filled basket on the table between them. "I don't know. I've even provided the evidence to my colleagues, and they haven't seen anything quite like it." A small grimace pulled on the skin around his eyes as he pushed himself from the ground and sat in one of the armchairs. "I believe we are looking at a creature that hasn't existed in a long time. Decades—perhaps even centuries. We don't have much information in our files. I will need to get closer. Gather more evidence." He paused as if contemplating. "I need to see this creature myself to figure out what it is."

"No!" she cried, thinking of how the ghoul had protected her, how he had spoken to her softly and touched her with such tenderness. But when La Cour lifted an eyebrow, she backtracked, "If it's a creature that hasn't existed in a long time, one that is fast enough and smart enough to evade the authorities, perhaps you shouldn't get involved."

The statement didn't have its intended effect, not when the detective's mouth lifted in a smirk, and he leaned forward on his cane to pierce her with an intense, knowing stare.

"You care about my well-being, Miss Thompson? Well, perhaps my flowers *were* well-received."

She returned his smirk with a scowl. "Except for the part where they lay mangled in a basket. You still have not told me the truth. What do you want from me?"

His eyes sparked with a burning fire filled with amusement and perhaps a bit of excitement. "Not easy to woo, hmm? I can't resist a challenge."

"There is nothing to challenge. Now why are you here? The vampire-bite patient still hasn't woken. You may check on him, if you'd like."

"Yes, I would like to. We'll have to adhere to decorum later."

"Mmhmm. The decorum of tea, which you may or may not drink depending on your mood."

"Yes." He grinned. "That one."

This time, she allowed him to lead, as he seemed to know his way around already. His slight limp drew her attention as they ventured down the hallway, and curiosity got the best of her.

"How did you hurt your leg?" she asked hesitantly, not knowing whether it was a sensitive subject.

He frowned. "An assignment gone wrong, I believe."

"You don't know for sure?"

For a moment, it was almost as if his soul left his body the way he stared forward with a tortured expression. As if he were somewhere other than the present. "I do not wish to speak of it."

"Very well."

Despite how the detective seemed to enjoy the sound of his own voice, he certainly was quite a mystery. A leg injury from an assignment gone wrong. A kiss with a demon that she suspected wasn't actually from a *demon*. She wasn't entirely sure *what* to believe about him.

When they stepped into the infirmary, the heavy scent of metal startled her eyes wide open. She rushed toward the vampire-bite patient and threw open his privacy curtain.

The man was ripped open and covered in his own blood. His eyes stared vacantly at the ceiling, hardly discernible against the flecks of red on his face.

She didn't need to take his pulse to know he was dead.

"I don't understand!" she gasped. "I checked on him this morning! He was still alive a couple hours ago." When she remembered he was a detective working on the Whitechapel police force, she spun toward La Cour. "I didn't do this, I swear! I have alibis. My sisters and patients can surely confirm my whereabouts. And…"

Her words trailed off when he bent at the waist. He clutched his stomach with one hand while the other clamped over his mouth. "I think I'm going to be sick."

"Pardon? You're supposed to be a detective. How can you not stand the sight of a little blood?"

"A little?" he squeaked. "This is more than just a little. Besides, I must first mentally prepare myself beforehand. I am not currently prepared."

Before she managed another word, he stumbled toward the waste bin resting against the wall and vomited inside. Perhaps her first instinct should have been to comfort him and provide him with medicine to help quell his queasiness, but she couldn't help but stare in shock. For someone who dealt with scenarios such as this on an ongoing basis, he was certainly overreacting.

"Who could have done this?" she murmured, turning from him entirely to examine what was left of the patient. This time, it was messy unlike the other Jack the Ripper killings. Messy and uncontrolled. Directionless. Had the ghoul done this? But the victim was a man and not a woman, so it couldn't be true.

Could it?

Detective La Cour approached with a handkerchief covering his mouth, his face a pale shade of green. After a moment, he shook his head. "This wasn't done by the Ripper. This was something else."

After the whirlwind of a day she'd had, Clara was surprised to find the night quiet and still.

She sat in a rocking chair on the back porch and stared blearily into the darkness, fighting the exhaustion raging within her burning eyes. Over the last several hours, police had been in and out of the house, questioning her and her sisters, her patients, searching for evidence, carting the body away and cleaning the bloody mess.

And only now that everyone had left and the few patients who had chosen to stay lay asleep, the shock dissolved into long-awaited fear.

Someone or *something* had been in her house. Torn up a body. Killed someone. That someone could have been her or Mazie or Norma. But rather… It felt like some sort of message. A threat.

But a threat to stop the investigation? A warning that she was being watched? Or perhaps it was a promise. If she stepped out of line, she would meet the same fate.

Knowing full well that she might fall asleep if she remained sitting and place herself in danger, she pushed herself to her feet and leaned against the scratchy wooden railing circling the porch. At one point, it had been smooth and flawless. But now? It was a shoddy display of the lack of upkeep on the property, a reminder that this house wasn't what it once was and would never return to its original splendor.

Crickets chirped in a unified song in the darkness. Moonlight danced across the overgrown lawn. The scent of midnight blooms opening their petals to the darkness filled their air. Quiet. Peaceful.

At least until the crickets ceased chirping all too suddenly, and the temperature seemed to drop ten degrees.

She spun around and backed up but failed to spot the stairs in the darkness. Her foot slipped on the edge of the top stair, and she couldn't help but shriek as she fell backward. In a single moment, she felt the wind in her hair as her stomach dropped, and she braced herself for the impact against the ground.

But it never came.

Instead, a pair of strong hands caught her from behind, the long, black claws gentle against her elbows and a gust of breath parting the strands of hair that lay haphazardly against her chin.

A thrill shot through her just like it had in her bedroom, something between terror, intrigue, and excitement. It was addicting, this feeling. Being in immense danger but feeling safe and protected all at the same time.

"You must stop sneaking up on me!" she breathed, watching as the monster's hands flexed and relaxed against her arms. But then he spun her around quickly, barely giving her enough time to gasp in a breath of exhilaration before she found herself face to face with dark gray skin, wicked sharp teeth, and a yellow gaze so lethal that it could cut glass.

Those yellow eyes roamed over her face, her shoulders, her hair as if searching for something. She wasn't sure if he found it, either, when he took a step back while keeping his hands gripped around her forearms.

"You were in danger today," he murmured in a husky tone. "And I wasn't here to protect you."

The tightness in her chest eased when she realized it hadn't been him. He wasn't to blame for the bloody mess in her infirmary.

"Who did it?"

"If not for me?"

She bit her lip, all but confirming his question even with her silence. If he ripped open prostitutes to keep the contagion from spreading, surely, he wasn't above accomplishing the task on her property, either.

"I don't know." He shook his head. "Well, I suspect… But it's not easy to prove. They mutilated the body. Made it look like my work. But I didn't do it. You must believe me."

"You have never lied to me thus far." At least, not that she knew of.

Foolish girl! she internally berated herself. This was a terrible idea. She should back away. Run to the house and lock herself inside. And then for good measure, she should lock all the windows to bar entrance from outsiders. Who knew just how many inhuman creatures had crossed the threshold of her home?

Two, at the very least. She wasn't sure she wanted to know the exact amount, either.

"I have something for you," he murmured, almost shyly. His eyebrows drew together. One of his sharp teeth peeked through his mouth and rested against his dark gray lip. The pointed curves on his back flattened against his spine. Whereas someone might have found him intimidating, she thought him subdued and sweet like a puppy wanting attention.

What is the matter with me? she silently berated herself. These...these...*feelings*...should not be making a nest within her chest and settling down in the warm heat. Any sane person would have run.

But she didn't want to run. She wanted to learn more about him.

"What is it?" she whispered, only realizing he still held onto her the moment he released one of his hands and reached behind his back. Instinct caused her to shift away. But rather than producing a weapon or something equally dangerous, he pulled out a single flower.

A beautiful, symmetrical red camellia. It said far more than words could, as it represented longing and affection. And he presented it to *her* with gentle fingers and an uncertain curve to his mouth.

When fluster burned her body even hotter than before, she took the flower from him and breathed a chuckled sigh. "Where on earth were you hiding this? In your trousers?"

And then her face flamed when she realized what, exactly, had escaped her mouth in her fluster.

His mouth lifted in a sharp, toothy grin. "My back pocket. I saw what became of your other flowers, and, well…"

She planted a hand on her hip. "Have you been watching me?"

"You looked so sad."

Another pang beat against her chest, and she frowned as she glanced back toward the house. From here, she could peer into her drawing room if she wanted to. It would have been easy for the ghoul to do the same even without her knowing. "Why are you watching me?"

She glanced down at the flower, unable to help herself as she cradled it protectively in her hands. Mazie couldn't destroy this one. She wouldn't let her.

His gravelly voice sounded only a step behind her. "I worried the vampires would target you after what happened. I don't mean to scare you. I just wanted to keep you safe."

"Why?" But as she gazed down at the flower, she realized his romantic intentions. However, she didn't truly understand his reasons. "I'm just a nurse."

"A nurse who took on two vampires and bravely landed a couple hits. I know none other with your mettle."

A pause settled between them, and she took that moment to brush her thumb over one of the soft, velvety petals of the camellia.

He coughed. "That, and you're my fated mate."

"Pardon?" she shrieked, spinning around to face him once more.

He rubbed the back of his neck and stared up at the sky rather than at her, and for a moment, she wondered if she'd misheard.

It couldn't be true. She hardly knew the ghoul. Besides, she'd only recently learned monsters were real. This made little sense.

A long breath escaped him before his yellow gaze honed in on her. He stalked forward slowly, and she stepped backward. At least until her shoulders bumped against the porch railing behind her, and he trapped her against the wooden slats.

"Your scent drives me wild," he murmured. From any other person, the tone could have been sultry, but his ghoul voice leaked gravel and husk in a way that sent shivers up her spine. Pleasant shivers.

"I-I-I'm not—" she stammered, unable to look away from the intensity of his gaze.

His tail looped around and caressed her face from her temple to her cheek to her chin. Leathery and soft and gentle. Enough for gooseflesh to crawl across her skin and meet the burn raging hotter in her soul.

"I knew it the moment I saw you in that alleyway." He leaned closer and skimmed the tip of his nose along her throat, inhaling her scent. She gasped. "You are *mine*. And I refuse to allow a vampire to lay their hands on you ever again."

"We only just met," she jested, surprisingly without a stammer. It was difficult to think, let alone form words, when he touched her so tenderly and spoke so softly. "You cannot say such things."

Besides, he wasn't the only one vying for her attention. Shockingly.

As if attuned to the direction of her thoughts, he leaned back, his tail swishing back and forth in agitation.

"You are not going to court him, are you?" His upper lip lifted in a snarl. "The detective."

"It's not a good idea."

"Why?"

"It's causing contention in my home." She glanced down at the flower in her hand, realizing another reason she hesitated. Detective La Cour was every woman's fancy. Handsome. Sophisticated. Successful. And she suspected to some degree that he might be wealthy or at least come from a well-off background. Why would someone like him set his sights on someone like her?

"Is there any other reason?" The corner of his mouth lifted in a smirk. "Perhaps that you might actually like ghouls more than you thought."

She laughed but then quickly clamped a hand over her mouth, glancing up at the windows high above her. The window belonging to her sister remained lit by the lanterns within, but no shadows or silhouettes passed across the light, and no windows opened, either.

"Fine," she relented, surprising even herself when she gently pushed his shoulder. But the toned physique beneath her hand gave her pause. The ghoul was solid muscle, all hardness and shape. Almost like stone. But not a gargoyle.

A blush stole across her cheeks as she dropped her hand and stammered, "P-p-perhaps they're not as terrifying as I previously imagined when standing on this side of the line."

"And what side is that?" he asked softly.

Until now, she hadn't realized how close he was. Towering over her. Shielding her with his body. A safe presence rather than something to shy away from.

A shaky exhale escaped her mouth. "The side on which he looks at me with such tenderness in his eyes."

His claws curled as he lifted his hand and caressed the back of his fingers over her cheek, almost like the whisper of a breeze on her skin.

"Is it too much to hope for," he murmured with the faintest exhale, "that you might accept a kiss from a ghoul?"

Clara's heart pounded as she gazed back into the yellow of his eyes. Her pulse thrummed at her neck, at her wrists, in her ears. Heat flashed across her body. He was a ghoul. A creature of the night. A formidable monster lurking in the shadows. But he was also gentle. He protected her from threats. He saw *her* in a way no one else did.

Perhaps she might feel a little tenderness, too.

"Would I be entirely unhinged if I didn't outright refuse?" she whispered, taking the smallest step forward and bracing her hand against his solid chest.

"Perhaps a little bit," he jested, but he wasted no more time as his fingers curled around her head. There was the briefest pause like the quiet before a clap of thunder. And then he closed the distance between them.

Their lips touched in a scalding kiss as hot as a forest fire, as if the lightning brewing between them had struck the ground and started an inferno. The flames were wild. Untamed. Full of life and vigor and strength. It was as if his key unlocked something within her with the faintest *click*. And she knew. She *knew*. The ghoul was correct. There was something between them she couldn't quite explain. Something heavy. Significant. And overall *right*.

As his arms moved down to circle her waist, inspiring warmth and happiness she never thought possible, she believed him. She believed she could be his mate, no matter how ludicrous that sounded. Perhaps she was so desperate for love that she would accept it even from a monster.

Or perhaps...

Perhaps this was where she was meant to be all along. All those years alone. All those years brushed off because of her profession, because of her sister. They were worth it just for this moment.

With a ghoul of all people.

Only a short time ago, she hadn't known they'd existed. And now?

And now, her hands smoothed over the muscles of his chest, the strength of his shoulders, the burliness of his arms. His embrace tightened around her, and the sigh that escaped him weakened her knees enough for her to have to rely on his strength to keep her from losing her balance entirely.

What a fool she was.

But for once, she enjoyed playing the fool. Because nothing could be better than his kiss, than his arms holding her safe and tight.

"I will never let you get hurt," he whispered against her lips, kissing her again and again until it was all she could do just to remain on her feet. "I will protect you with my every breath."

"That's a hefty promise," she said in a gasping voice as his lips moved to her jaw, her throat, and then back to her lips, "for someone who burns in the sunlight."

A deep chuckle resounded in his chest, and in response, his tail wrapped around her, holding her closer still. "I am not a vampire, love."

"Then what happens to you?"

His lips skimmed over her ear, and a delightful shiver ran through her body when she felt his sharp yet gentle teeth brush against her neck. She wanted more. So much more. If the fool was now her guide, then she would wholeheartedly play the role to her best ability.

"I sleep," he answered. "A heavy sleep. I cannot fight it."

He hovered over her mouth, tantalizingly close. She desperately wanted to close the gap between them, but he was far too tall, especially when holding himself at bay.

"Then how did you witness the incident in the drawing room?"

He chuckled again. "My sleep is not always so heavy."

There was so much to learn about him, so much to discover. But rather than asking more questions, rather than kissing him well into the night until the dawn made its appearance in the sky, they froze when the sound of a window opening threatened to expose their position in the yard.

The ghoul took her hand and quietly guided her to the side of the estate where they hid in the shadows. Disappointment dropped her heart to her stomach when, instead of kissing her again, he spoke in a low, rushed whisper.

"I need your help. I wouldn't ask this of you if there was any other way."

She nodded mutely, rather distracted by the pleasant tingling sensation on her lips.

He continued, "The man who was killed in your home… The police will undoubtedly trace him back to me. They'll search harder. It will put them in danger. It will put *me* in danger." The deep breath he released shifted loose strands of hair around her face. "I need the police report destroyed. It won't stop the investigation, but it will hinder it. Long enough for me to put a dent in the vampire coven."

When his words finally sank past the haze created from his kiss alone, she blinked several times and bit her lip. "You cannot go after these vampires. They are dangerous."

"I know." He sighed. "But they still have vials left of my blood. They must be stopped."

Shaking her head, she tried to wrap her mind around the danger. Especially after what she'd witnessed in the alleyway. "Why not destroy the documents yourself?"

"I would if I could. Believe me, I would never ask this of you otherwise." He lifted a strand of her hair with one of his claws and delicately brought it to his nose, inhaling what must be her scent. Her cheeks warmed at the thought. "Like vampires, I can only prowl the night, and they are expecting me to do this. They are expecting me to go after the documents. The police station is surrounded. It would be an ambush." He lifted his gaze to meet her eye. "But *you*… You can go during the day."

She quickly shook her head. "But I don't have a way in—" Her words ceased suddenly, and her eyes widened when she realized that wasn't true. "You want me to abuse my connection with the detective."

"I wouldn't ask otherwise," he repeated, running a claw up and down her arm.

The sensation of warmth and tingles were far too pleasant to resist, and she couldn't help but lean into his touch. At the same time, she wondered what was wrong with her. He was a ghoul. A monster. This wasn't supposed to be something a sane person enjoyed.

"The detective is a good man," she accused. "I cannot trick him like this."

"I'm sure he would understand."

"I don't think he would. This is his livelihood on the line."

"He is hunting me. He would be walking into something even he cannot handle. Choosing between his livelihood and his life... What do you think he would pick if he truly understood?"

She stared at the ground with a troubled expression when she realized the ghoul was right. Claude La Cour would be walking straight into a dangerous situation, and she wasn't sure she would be able to make him listen long enough to stop him, the stubborn man that he was.

Especially if she told him she'd received all her information from a very convincing ghoul.

"At least tell me your name," she whispered, realizing she had no idea what to call him.

His sharp, toothy grin lifted at the corner of his lips. "For now, just call me Jack."

The name sent a chilling thrill down her spine when she realized he referred to his "stage name." But then she internally scoffed at the idea. Jack was trying to do something good. It was only a shame no one truly understood.

He left her with a lingering parting kiss, enough for her knees to grow weak and her lungs to become breathless. And then she watched as he slipped into the shadows and disappeared from sight.

After a moment, she brought her fingers to her lips where his kiss still tingled in a pleasant manner. And then she realized something entirely mad and nutty.

She liked Jack the Ripper far more than she should.

Chapter Nine

Very little could make Clara's heart pound harder than walking toward the police station with a large secret on her shoulder and the weight of guilt on her mind. For all she knew, vampires could be watching somewhere from the shadows, unable to leap out at her because of the sunlight. She made sure to always keep one foot in the sunlight, going the long way around a building or two if only to keep out of the shadows.

Jack's life might depend on her success today.

It was only a shame Claude had to be caught in the crossfire.

As she neared the large square building, she hesitated when a young boy waved a newspaper in his hand on the opposite side of the street, calling out to passersby to buy a copy of…

The Star.

It was as if her feet reacted on their own as she closed the remaining distance between them, shoved a penny into the boy's hand, and made off with the newspaper.

Sure enough, front and center lay an image of a figure cloaked in shadows, the artist making the man large and bulky with a knife held in each hand. The headline read: *The Ripper Strikes Again!*

Her eyes flew over the article, but then she dropped it to her side in disgust. It depicted the murder from the infirmary, the very one the Ripper had *not* committed. Thankfully, they hadn't publicly disclosed the location of the murder, otherwise, people might be glancing her way.

They didn't.

"What a waste of an article," she muttered under her breath before tucking the newspaper beneath her arm. "I want my money returned."

Unfortunately, even if she tried, the boy would never agree to it. They carried their money tighter than a woman's corset when trying to catch a husband.

Deciding not to stare at the police building any longer, she tightened her grip on the handle of her basket and marched inside as if she belonged there when in reality, her heart pounded hard in her chest, and a part of her felt as if she might vomit.

She was nervous. Why? She wasn't entirely sure. But what she *did* know was she had never done something like this before—actively pursue a man even if it were under false pretenses like her own. Surely, Detective La Cour would figure out her game long before she managed to destroy those documents.

The police office was a hubbub of male voices, flipping papers, and whining civilians, giving an orderly chaos sort of atmosphere the moment she stepped inside the building. Several office doors were closed on the opposite side of the large room, though she managed to catch a glimpse of civilians and officers through the windows. Several rows of long desks lay in the center of the room with stacks of papers and folders, each filled with young men working hard to impress their boss, no doubt.

But what she didn't find? The detective himself. Was he out researching the case? Had she missed him entirely? During lunch hour, she thought she would find him here of all places.

"Clara!" someone gasped behind her, and she spun around to find the detective in question staring at her with an open mouth as if she'd just flashed him an ankle. He held a mug in his hand filled with brown liquid she highly suspected was coffee, and it took all her restraint not to steal it from him and down the entire thing in a few gulps.

He'd probably let her, too.

The corner of her lips lifted in amusement. "Detective."

"W-w-what are you doing here?" He hurried to fix his hair and pulled down his white sleeves until they covered his forearms. "And please, call me Claude."

Her grin only grew wider. "Am I not allowed to visit you at work? Claude." She tasted his given name in her mouth, though it felt foreign on her tongue as if she'd sampled a piece of chocolate she had not had the chance of enjoying in a long while.

She glanced toward the desks lined up in the room to find men staring at her as if she'd just flashed an ankle toward them, too. Each snapped their attention back to their work, though she acutely felt their focus on her, nonetheless.

When he still fussed with his clothing, she asked, "Is there a time when you are *not* drinking coffee? It's the afternoon. Do you get any sleep at all?"

"It certainly feels like I don't." He chuckled, and she didn't resist in the slightest as he handed over his mug, and she took it eagerly from his fingers.

Because…she hadn't gotten much sleep, either. What with the murder in her home, Mazie's accusations and acts of revenge, and Jack's earth-rattling kiss. Not to mention the patients who still relied on her for their health.

What a mess, she thought to herself. How had she managed to find herself in this situation?

Again, her gaze passed over the police officers pretending to work. One even scribbled over one of his papers, but no ink touched the surface. "Is this what you do all day?" She turned a teasing grin toward the detective. "Aside from staring at corpses and bothering young nurses, of course."

His mouth twitched at her jest before he nodded his head toward the hallway. He turned on his heel and led her down the corridor, and she followed, overly aware of a half-dozen pairs of eyes following her every movement. It was almost as if they'd never seen a woman before. However, judging by how much *Claude* worked, she could rightfully assume some, if not many, of the other officers worked hours enough to keep them from the opposite sex as well.

He led her into a dark room at the end of the hallway and pulled open the shutters. She blinked in surprise at the sudden sunlight entering through the window. But then she froze when she noticed the *walls*.

Nearly every little piece of space on the walls was tacked with articles, pictures, strings, and everything in between, including a swath of gray fabric. It was as if everything was interconnected in the most bizarre fashion if the room was any indication.

"That does it," she murmured, eyes wide as she turned in a full circle. "I suspected you were insane before, but this makes it official. I'm leaving. And I'm taking your coffee with me."

She turned toward the door, but Claude quickly caught her by the elbow, laughing as he pulled her back into the room. "It's not as bad as it appears," he defended himself with a grin spread across his face. "I swear."

Lifting an eyebrow, she surveyed the mess of strings appearing to lead nowhere and everywhere at once. "I beg to differ."

She ducked her head beneath a particularly low-hanging string and surveyed the pin-cushion board littered with images and articles. Surprisingly, Claude didn't stop her from rubbing the gray cloth between her fingers.

And then her veins froze over with ice when she recognized it as belonging to one of those vampires who had attacked her in the alleyway. It was the same material as the neckcloth he'd worn.

Coincidence? Or not?

"What is this?" she breathed, turning her head away to avoid revealing her thoughts.

Claude glanced toward the open door before lowering his voice. "We found blood in an alleyway. Only this was left behind."

Her fingers shook around the mug of coffee, and she brought the warm liquid to her lips to try to hide it. "You think it belongs to the Ripper?"

"I don't know." He ran a hand over his chin and glanced from the door to his board. "The blood belonged to a vampire, but the Ripper's attacks don't coincide with that of a vampire. I'm not yet sure how this connects—if it does at all."

"Did you—" She cleared her throat. "Did you find anything else?"

Such as something that might implicate her as well. Or even Jack.

"Fragments of wood. Chipped brick. Vampire blood. This swath of fabric. Not enough evidence to connect this to the Ripper, but every bit is worth investigating."

For a moment, she studied his tall, slender profile as he stared at the board with crossed arms, a puzzled frown on his face. He was insistent and dedicated to this case. Jack was right. If she couldn't convince Claude to step away, she must destroy the documents to hinder his progress.

But where were they?

The mess of folders, parchment, and paperweights on the desk discouraged her, as she'd never find the files she needed within the chaos. Claude La Cour was a disorderly man. Who would have known? Especially judging by his often-neat appearance alone.

"What are you telling the other officers?" she murmured, now her turn to glance toward the door.

He crossed to the desk, dug through a pile, and picked up a folder before opening it. Her heart leaped to her throat as she approached slowly, hope blossoming within her. Was this *the* folder with *the* documents? Had he just shown her what she must inevitably destroy?

"Everything is written in code," he answered, flipping through several documents. "Should another officer look through my findings, it will appear normal. But there may be a monster and a few vampires involved. Probably." He winked at her, which did strange things to her stomach as it flipped and flopped and fluttered.

It's only because he's handsome, she tried to convince herself. *He likely flirts with any woman he comes across.*

"Do you often deal with vampires?" she ventured.

"Why?" he asked, and she watched a little too closely as he set the folder back on the table and crossed his arms to look her way. "Are you worried about me?"

She detected the flirty hint of amusement in his tone. This was her chance to do what needed to be done or to flee entirely and abandon her original quest.

But as she thought of Jack, a desire to protect him surfaced. She wanted to keep him safe, even if that meant deceiving a detective.

"Yes," she answered truthfully, which seemed to take him entirely off guard.

He dropped his hands to his sides, and his lips parted as he stared at her with an unreadable expression. The longer he stared, the more her stomach fluttered. She couldn't stand it. Because what she was about to do was sure to hurt him if—or perhaps *when*—he found out.

"Umm," she said to break the silence in the room. "These are for you."

She lifted the corners of a cloth from her basket, which harbored a dozen biscuits within, and placed them on top of the desk, making sure to leave the remaining cloth inside for when she would need it soon.

"Biscuits?" His eyebrows lifted nearly to his hairline. "I didn't know you baked."

"I don't." She laughed and shook her head in a self-deprecating manner. "Norma made these. I hardly have extra time to visit you here, let alone stand in front of the kitchen for hours on end."

"Then I feel very fortunate, indeed, that you chose to spend what little time you have by paying me a visit."

"Ah, well, you've taken time out of your busy day to stop by the infirmary. I could at least show a little appreciation for the flowers." She smiled as she took another sip from the mug. "And for the coffee."

He shifted a little closer, and she swore he would be able to hear the way her heart pounded should he only lean forward the slightest bit.

"I can now see that flowers were not the right gift for you." He smirked, his gaze flickering to the mug in her hands. "Seeing as you do enjoy hoarding my coffee."

She laughed and shook her head sadly. "Coffee has turned into a want rather than a need. I cannot purchase it any longer. So, I will take yours any chance I get."

Oh no. Was she flirting back?

Not at all. This was necessary for her task for the Ripper. It meant nothing. Therefore, she could either distract him or seek a reason for him to leave her alone with the documents. But she must make a quick choice.

However, she realized the choice was already made for her when Claude took another step toward her until his tall frame towered over her, highlighting the amusement shining in the blue of his eyes. Amusement and…

Something else.

Interest. Passion. She wasn't sure. But did she really want to find out?

"Now I see the real reason you visit me," he jested. "You only like me for my coffee."

"You caught me," she replied, but the sudden frog in her throat caused the words to escape as a rasp.

This was a terrible idea, getting caught up in this. By going out that night and getting cornered by vampires, she had involved herself in something big and could do nothing other than see it through.

Even if it meant deceiving a detective with her less-than-wily charms. She'd never had to attempt to charm a man, but it appeared as if she hardly needed to make the effort with Claude.

He leaned closer until his fingers skimmed over the fabric of her sleeve. Momentary panic crashed into her when she realized exactly what she'd encouraged. Not only that, but what must be done.

She cared for Jack. He was not the monster everyone thought he was. He deserved a chance to accomplish his admirable goals without the risk of a knife to his throat no matter which way he turned.

Therefore, she would help give him whatever chance he needed to succeed.

She set the mostly empty coffee mug aside and focused her attention on Claude. Her fingers ceased trembling. Her pounding heart stilled. Calm replaced her previous fear and uncertainty as she responded to his hesitant touch by leaning against the corner of his desk and moving her foot to rest against his.

As if bolstered by the action, he more daringly cupped her elbow. His thumb caressed her arm. "Am I in the wrong to believe you stopped by because...well...because I hold some form of your affection?"

Her throat seemed to close up, making speaking difficult when he looked at her like *that*. With hopeful eyes and a hesitant twist of his mouth. Like he would be absolutely crushed should she reject him.

"You don't skirt around, do you?" she whispered.

"Not one bit."

He stepped impossibly closer, his hand now resting on her waist rather than her arm. But he stopped advancing and tipped his head to the side as if in question. Giving her a chance to push him away, to reject him and slip out of the room.

If this was the only way to help Jack *and* Claude, then she refused to stop now.

In a quick movement, she wrapped her leg around his and pulled him closer. He gasped in surprise moments before their lips collided in a kiss.

What she hadn't expected were the accompanying emotions.

They flashed past so quickly that it was difficult to grasp onto one long enough to make sense of any of it. All she knew was she hadn't expected to kiss him. And she hadn't expected to want more.

Her grip on his leg tightened as she pulled him even closer, sparking an unexpected passion growing wild between them. His arms looped around her until one of his hands held the back of her neck and the other cupped behind her knee. A whirlwind of heat and joy and panic consumed her until she might as well have forgotten her own name when her mind momentarily refused to work.

She had to stop this. She had to get out of there.

With what little remained of her self-control, she shifted on the desk, purposefully knocking files and folders to the floor.

"Sorry," she gasped.

"I don't care."

More parchment fell to the floor, his doing this time, as he swiped a hand across the surface to make room for her to sit more fully on the desk. Her stomach fluttered. Her blood burned. And for a moment, she wanted to throw everything to the ground to make room for *both* of them.

At least until the muffled laughter down the corridor reminded her of where they were, and that they weren't alone.

She pushed him away and gasped, her face flaming with the heat of fluster. "I can't… This is not the best… Someone will see…" She shook her head and stooped down to where the piles of folders and parchment lay scattered across the ground. "I'll help you clean this up."

"No, no, no. It's not necessary." He stooped next to her and gathered papers into his hands. "I can do it."

He turned his back for the briefest moment, and she took that opportunity to snatch the Ripper files, stuff them into her basket, and cover them with the extra cloth she'd brought. She had to make a timely escape before he noticed.

"I-I-I'm sorry," she stuttered, unable to look at him without her cheeks burning. She didn't even have to feign fluster, unfortunately. "I-I-I have to go. My patients… And Norma…"

Not giving him a chance to reply, she spun on her heel and walked quickly out of the room and down the empty corridor. As she entered the main room, she was sure everyone must have noticed her flushed face and the way she smoothed down her hair as dozens of eyes trailed her departure.

She had not expected this to happen. This was not good. Not good at all.

Gasping in a breath of fresh air the moment she stepped outside, she leaned against the cold bricks of the building as she tried to catch her breath. Because Claude had stolen it. And she didn't know if she could get it back.

She paused, doubting herself as she glanced down at the basket in her hands. Claude was a good man. Deceiving him like this tore her heart in several different directions. This was wrong. But what about Jack? She had growing feelings for the ghoul. He *and* Claude could get hurt if she didn't help and do what he'd asked of her.

But Claude...

Indecision warred within her as she bit her knuckle. She liked both Jack *and* Claude. It was impossible not to. She could not be courting two men. What would Jack do when he found out what happened today?

First things first. She had to burn the documents. And then she would figure out what to do from there.

Chapter Ten

Clara knew she'd made a mess of things. She just didn't know how bad until she hadn't heard from Claude for days, which turned into a week. And she hadn't seen an inkling of Jack, either.

"What is wrong with me?" she murmured to herself, running a hand down her cheek after a long day. She'd never been so focused on men in her life. They distracted her from her patients and earning the living her family desperately needed, and they distracted her now. She needed to focus. No more fantastical thoughts or wayward emotions.

And certainly, no more men.

She released a long sigh as she tidied up the newest available cot in the infirmary, placing supplies in the drawer and smoothing down clean sheets with her hand. The cot would be filled by tomorrow, without a doubt. They never stayed empty for long.

Behind her, the curtain drew open and closed with a hiss. Clara spun around, one hand to her heart while she reached for a scalpel with the other. But before her fingers closed around the small item, her arm dropped to her side in shock.

The Ripper stood a few paces away, his arm wrapped around his torso while his chest heaved with each labored breath he took. Thick, black liquid coated his hands and dripped between his fingers, and only then did she realize what it was.

Blood.

"Jack!" she gasped, abandoning her fear to rush toward him. Concern pushed out any previous caution as she pulled his hand away just enough to reveal the deep gash in his torso and the blood spilling out.

She thrust a wadded cloth onto the wound and instructed him to apply pressure while she hastily sifted through her medical supplies located in the drawer beside the empty cot. The wound appeared deep, and a part of her feared he might either bleed out or faint from blood loss if she moved too slowly. The heavens only knew she couldn't lift his massive body enough to move him somewhere safe and discreet before the police found him and killed him on sight.

"Clara!" Norma shouted from the opposite side of the room. She froze. "Where are the extra bandages? I thought we ordered more last week."

Taking a deep breath, Clara answered as calmly as possible while maintaining eye contact with Jack's yellow, beastly eyes, "I haven't had the chance to put them away. They're still in the crate."

Several moments passed with Clara holding her breath, hoping her sister would stay away from the curtain.

But then Norma replied, "Ah! Found them. Mrs. Griffon is in need of a change of bandages. If you are busy, I think I can manage it."

Busy? Jack mouthed with the quirk of his brow and the faintest smirk on his lips despite the evident agony in his expression.

She pointed a finger at him and mouthed back, *I will smack you.*

And then she cleared her throat to answer, "I appreciate the help, Norma. I have to see to a patient, but then I'll return shortly."

Or perhaps not so shortly. It was a bad wound.

Realizing she couldn't perform the stitches in the infirmary without putting Norma at risk of finding out about the Ripper, she snatched Jack's hand and slipped out of the curtain when her sister's back was turned and rushed down the hallway into the darker corridor leading into the private section of the estate.

Jack followed behind without a single complaint, his labored steps the only indication of his discomfort.

In a sudden, disorienting movement, Jack took her by the waist, spun her quick enough for wind to whip through her hair, and pinned her quietly against the wall in the corner of the hallway where the darkest shadows lingered.

Her breath hitched. Heat flushed through her body at his sudden nearness. No, it most certainly wasn't fear coursing through her veins. It was excitement. Anticipation.

And...

Oh, dear.

She'd made a mess of things. She needed to tell him about what had happened with Claude.

"Jack," she whispered, afraid to disturb the stillness of the moment as her hand came to rest on the sturdy muscles of his chest. But as she lifted her head to meet his eye, she found him staring intensely at the wall instead. "I need to tell you—"

"Hush." He placed a finger to her lips, and that's when she made out the sound of quiet footsteps.

Mazie turned the corner, dressed in day clothes despite the late hour with a shawl and bonnet to match. She held her boots in her hands, walking the estate with only stockinged feet as if not wanting to get caught.

Although she was coming rather than going, she was still returning home two hours past dark. And the night was dangerous.

Clara attempted to push away from Jack to confront Mazie, but he shook his head and held her still as her sister slipped past and tiptoed down the hallway. After a few moments, the door to Mazie's bedroom clicked shut. She hadn't even seen them. But then again, it was difficult to see Jack in the darkness.

"She's been going out on her own!" Clara hissed, gesturing down the hallway. "At night. What if…what if…" A shuddering breath escaped her as she envisioned what could happen. Would Jack have to *deal* with her, too, should the vampires infect her?

Frantically turning her attention back to him, she said, "You can't hurt her. If she gets infected, you can't kill her. Promise me. Promise me!"

"Nothing will happen," he murmured, shifting a strand of hair out of her face with his claw. "I will deal with these vampires, and the streets will be a little bit safer."

The reminder of the vampires brought her attention back to his wound. Not wanting him to suffer and bleed out any longer, she grabbed his hand, led him down the opposite end of the hallway, and ushered him through her bedroom door.

She struck a tinderbox and lit a lantern, illuminating the room enough to view his wound. It was deep. But perhaps not so deep that he would suffer from internal damage.

Immediately, she got to work as she snatched the chair in front of her vanity and ushered him to sit. His vast size in her little chair amused her, especially when he looked entirely out of place.

Next, she set out clean cloths, a sterilized needle, catgut thread, and carbolic acid as a disinfectant. She threw on an apron and hastily tied it at the back before slipping on rubber gloves. Growing up, her father had never used gloves, as it had not become a practice for physicians until later. But if she could keep her hands clean and her patients safe, she would take whatever precautions necessary.

Besides, if Jack's blood was capable of infecting women through consumption, she couldn't dare risk even the slightest bit touching her lips or even the smallest open wound.

"You certainly know what you're doing." Jack grunted, the skin around his eyes crinkling as he winced.

"I may have done this once or twice," she jested as she sat in front of him and began cleaning the wound with water and a cloth. The water was cold, straight from her basin. But she couldn't risk boiling a pot downstairs lest Norma catch her in the act. It was better to avoid questions altogether.

But as she cleaned the blood away, she frowned at what she found. The wound was straight enough to suggest it had happened from some sort of blade, but slightly jagged to indicate it may not have been a clean, sharp, and well-kept weapon.

"You need to stay." After checking to make sure the skin was the only thing damaged, she began the first suture. His only indication of pain was a slight wince. "At least until you recover. I can help you here."

He shook his head. "I can't stay."

"Of course." She sighed and shook her head. "Demons to fight and vampires to slay. Am I wrong?" And then she nodded toward his wound. "Is that how you got this?"

She glanced up briefly to find him pressing his lips together in admittance. One of his sharp canines peeked through those lips. "I was ambushed. Perhaps I was not careful enough because they knew I was coming."

"This is a knife wound, Jack."

"And now they have more of my blood." His shoulders slumped with defeat. "There will be more victims. I'm afraid I won't be able to stop Whitechapel from being overrun with ghouls after all."

Silence fell between them as she performed her duties as a physician. Prick, tug. Prick, tug. Until slowly, the wound came together nicely, and the bleeding stopped. She finished tying off the last stitch and cut the catgut with scissors before applying the antiseptic paste, layering it on thick. He needed it after what he'd gone through.

After concluding her medical administration, she pinched his burly arm hard enough for him to gasp.

"Clara! Why did you—"

"I can't tell if you're brave or an idiot! They got more of your blood because you're still here. If you left the city, this wouldn't be an issue."

"Left this city?" he scoffed. He pushed himself to his feet and began pacing back and forth across the room while she packed her supplies away. "I can't leave. You don't understand."

"Why is the concept so difficult? Why, Jack?"

"Because!" He threw his hands up in the air and spun to face her. "Because you're here. And I refuse to leave you."

He moved so suddenly that she could hardly follow his movements with her eyes. One moment, he was across the room. And the next, he wrapped an arm around her waist, pinned her against the wall...

And kissed her.

This time, the burning inferno couldn't be contained between them. She lost all sense of time and place as the rightness of their bond seemed to click into place once again, and this time she wanted it to stay.

His deft claws pulled on the tie to her apron to loosen it before shrugging it over her head. And before she found a single moment to catch her breath, her hair fell around her shoulders after he took the pins out.

He pulled her flush against his body and kissed her neck. She gasped, bracing herself against his solid chest.

"I kissed Claude!" she said breathlessly, not wanting to keep it a secret from him. "To distract him to take the files. I kissed him. I'm sorry."

Instead of responding with anger, he chuckled against her throat, his lips moving from her jawline to her collarbone. "I don't care. But you're *mine* now."

The flicker of disappointment over the thought of never kissing Claude again after this vanished with the heat of Jack's warm lips on hers. His hands touched her gently but with a barely restrained passion, as if he wanted to be rougher but didn't want to hurt her.

Another gasp escaped her as he pinned her hands above her head against the wall, his chest heaving as he gazed down at her with a desire to match her own. Slowly, his tail snaked around her waist, the tip barely brushing against her cheek. It was sweet. Intimate. Impossible.

And she wanted more.

"I want to make you my mate in every sense of the word." His low, rumbling voice caressed her ears like a pleasant whisper. "Deny me now, and I will walk away. But if we go any farther, I don't think I can stop."

With her hands pinned, she couldn't touch him the way she wanted, so she settled on winding her leg around his and pulling him closer at the knee.

In an equal whisper, she replied, "Then make me yours."

Before the last word even left her mouth, he swooped her up in a quick movement until she rested inside his arms. It took all her willpower not to squeal in surprise. Instead, she clamped her mouth shut to prevent one of her sisters from hearing her. Honestly, she needn't have bothered when Jack's lips returned to hers, muffling each contented sigh and whispered word of affection.

She found herself hardly aware of her surroundings as the ghoul shuffled around the room in agile movements. The soft mattress of the bed met her back, momentarily snapping her out of her euphoria long enough to remember he was injured. They shouldn't be doing this. No matter how much either of them might want to.

"I just stitched you up." Her fingers lightly caressed his abdomen above the sutures. "Your doctor will not be happy should you tear them."

"I'll be careful."

"But your wound!"

"Is inconsequential to me compared to this." Sharp yet gentle claws caressed her face from temple to chin. "You are more important to me."

"You are insane," she breathed, enjoying the pleasant warmth his body offered from where it hovered over her.

A grin quirked at the corner of his mouth. "Then what does that make you?"

Her quiet laughter transitioned into a shuddering breath as his lips trailed across her collarbones, and as her dress loosened around her shoulders, between her breasts. Never in her life had she experienced such heat and warmth and desire. Being insane was the least of her worries, but she couldn't find a single care to back it.

A trail of simmering heat followed in the wake of his touch as his hands traveled over her arms, her waist, her legs, made hotter wherever his lips touched her skin.

Along with the desire to be touched, she wanted to explore him as well. Her fingers grazed the hard muscles of his arms, his shoulders, and then she more daringly buried her fingers into his black hair. His accompanying sigh gave her more courage to pull back on the dark strands to expose the cords of muscle on his neck. And when she brushed her lips along his throat, something between a whimper and a growl escaped his mouth.

"You will be the death of me, *mon amour*," he murmured with a wild look in his yellow eyes. "And I will walk into that death willingly if it means you will remain here in my arms."

"Stop talking about death," she laughed, smacking his arm. "It's morbid."

"I thought you enjoyed morbid things. Morbid or romantic, there's no telling with you."

The faintest memory sparked in her mind, but she couldn't latch on fast enough before Jack distracted her with another kiss. And then another. Until she fully lost herself in his touch, in the scent of him.

"Will this infect me?" she asked huskily, arms braced against his shoulders.

"If you drink my blood, then perhaps." A smirk grew across his face. "But even I am not that tarty."

She laughed, but the sound was promptly cut off by his kiss. A contented sigh escaped her as she wrapped her arms around his neck and arched her back to bring herself closer to him. This blossoming feeling inside of her... She dared not call it love, especially when she hardly understood it herself. But...

A smile broke free on her lips against his mouth. The thought most certainly occurred to her that this could bloom into something raw and beautiful and utterly romantic.

Yes, he may be a monster. But he was *her* monster. And nothing else mattered.

Chapter Eleven

There were two murders today.

The moment Clara picked up a copy of *The Star*, her stomach sank when she recognized Jack the Ripper's killing pattern within the article. The bodies were found in two different places within Whitechapel last night with similar wounds as the other victims, and one of them had been cut from breast to navel.

"Jack," she whispered, hand held to her mouth in disbelief as she stood in the infirmary with a bloody apron after an appendicitis surgery. "Please tell me you didn't do this."

She'd been with Jack last night. For a couple hours. Had he done this before or after they were intimate?

She shook her head and set the news article aside, nausea climbing up her esophagus for the first time in…well, a long time. Death and gore rarely affected her. But this? Knowing who was behind these murders? She needed an explanation.

Not now. Not tomorrow. She'd needed an explanation last night. Why hadn't Jack said something?

Why hadn't she asked?

Panic pounded through her veins. Dizziness spun her surroundings. And despite her bloodied apron, she sank onto a chair and focused on breathing deeply through her nose and releasing the breath from her mouth.

Mazie had been out last night. One of the women in the article could have ended up being her. Her sister was lucky. But next time? She might not be.

A rush of determination encompassed her as she leaped to her feet, tossed her bloodied apron aside, and rushed toward the front door just as Mazie stepped outside into the drizzling rain carrying an umbrella and a new pair of gloves. At least she thought they were new, as she had not seen them before.

Clara stepped into Mazie's path, and her sister released an annoyed huff. "You can't keep doing this! I know you've been sneaking out."

"That's none of your business!"

"It most certainly is my business!" She threw her hands up in exasperation. "There are things out there that are dangerous. You put me in a dither night after night when I can't help but worry for your safety." She ran a hand down her face, but it didn't erase the terrible worry plaguing her heart. "Where are you going every night? Are you entertaining men?"

Again, her gaze darted toward the gloves her sister wore. Unfortunately, Clara didn't give her sister enough pin money to afford such gloves. It was difficult enough to feed the three of them as it was.

Thunder rumbled across the skies overhead, and Mazie scowled as she adjusted her grip on her umbrella. "You told me to get a job, so I did. I work nights at The Ten Bells pub."

"But at night?"

Another huff. "Of course, you would disapprove. This is why I didn't want to speak of it." Her sister spun on her heel, and the pitter patter of rain hitting her umbrella filled the silence of her momentary shock before the drizzle transitioned into heavy sheets of moisture falling from the sky.

Mazie seemed to want so desperately to fly out of the coop, but didn't she realize this was dangerous?

Had she been too hard on her, regardless?

Realizing she still wore a single bloody rubber glove from her surgery, she slipped it off her hand, wadded it into a ball, and threw it into a waste bin inside the infirmary. She spent a long time scrubbing her hands with soap infused with rosemary until her skin turned red and her heart became numb with hurt and confusion. Thoughts of her sisters became prominent in her mind, and she couldn't help but wonder if she was handling the situation incorrectly.

In her youth, all she had ever wanted was to follow in her father's footsteps. She had worked hard to follow her dreams, and then both her parents had died, leaving her in charge of her sisters. Despite the strain on her shoulders, was she not allowing Mazie and Norma the same freedom and choices her parents had given her? Was her hold on them too tight?

She flicked the water off her hands before drying them on a cloth, but then she turned.

And froze.

A canister of coffee beans lay on the table across the room, and she wasn't sure whether to leap for joy or hide in the darkest corner of the estate from both mortification and despair. She could not court two men, even if one of them was a monster. Her *mate*, as he liked to call her.

She needed to let Claude down gently.

Why did the thought turn her stomach over with disappointment?

Slowly, she approached the canister and inspected it. The coffee beans within rattled as she turned it one way, and then the other. No note accompanied the gift, though she knew without a doubt who it was from.

The heady smell of the beans was enough to make her mouth salivate with the desire to consume it.

It was hardly fair that she needed to return it. Some gifts didn't come without strings, and she was sure this was one of them.

What a terrible shame. She liked Claude. She liked Jack as well. But she'd already made her choice. There was nothing more to be done.

Still, she held the canister tightly to her chest, not wanting to give it up yet as she made her way to the corridor leading to the drawing room. But she didn't take even five steps before a voice stopped her in her tracks. The deep timber of his French accent sent delightful shivers down her spine.

"Knowing you, the canister will be gone within the week."

Unable to help herself, Clara laughed, shaking her head as she turned toward Claude. "I can make it last longer than a week. For you on the other hand, this is only a day's worth…"

Her words trailed off when she found Claude leaning against the wall with one foot propped up behind him and his arms crossed over his chest. But it was the dark, tired shadows beneath his eyes that gave her pause. It was almost as if he hadn't slept the entire week of his absence, and not even coffee could fix it this time around.

"Claude!" she gasped as she took his hand and led him across the room, pushing him into a chair. He started to protest, but she shushed him with a finger to his lips.

She slipped a thermometer into his mouth, checked his pupil dilation using the light from a candle, and felt either side of his neck to check for abnormalities. Nothing seemed amiss. Even his temperature came back normal.

Perhaps only one thing could cause this.

"Go home and sleep," she said in the sternest tone she could manage. "Doctor's orders."

"I thought you needed a doctorate to be considered a doctor."

She glared at him and leaned closer, but her warning stare only caused him to chuckle and return her glare with amusement in his eyes.

"I cannot sleep on the job," he explained.

"Clearly, you are not sleeping at night, either, due to your obsession with this case. Your superiors can spare you for a few hours during the day."

"Obsession?" he scoffed. "This killer took two new victims only last night. I cannot afford to lose a single minute to unnecessary frivolities when people are dying."

He attempted to stand up, but she forcefully shoved him back into the chair and grabbed his stubbled chin to compel him to look into her eyes. "This is not your fault, Claude. You are not to blame for this."

"Aren't I? The way the officers look at me... I can feel their judgment through their stares. If I had only been quicker... I could have prevented this."

She shook her head, still holding onto his chin. "Those same officers were far more incompetent than you. Their judgment holds little flame when they had failed long before you."

Guilt pressed on her shoulders when she realized she knew far more than he did about his own case. Well, only as much as Jack had told her. But Jack had explicitly instructed her to discourage Claude's involvement, as he would only get himself killed.

However, she abhorred seeing him so downtrodden and hopeless.

"What have you been doing all this week?" she asked, slowly dropping her hand to her side. "I have not seen you in a while."

Claude scrubbed his hands over his face and hair, giving the strands a wild look to match his bloodshot eyes. "I misplaced the files for my case. I don't know what happened. They weren't where I last put them. Either I'm going insane, or there is a leak within the police force." He groaned into his hands. "I feel like my progress is only leading me backward."

She turned her back to him to hide the guilt filling every recess of her expression. She had done this to him. All she had wanted was to protect him. But how was this protecting him? Her trickery had caused hurt instead.

"I'm sorry," she said in a quavering tone, the apology having multiple meanings beyond his immediate comprehension.

"It's not your fault," he sighed.

Oh, if only he knew.

She wanted to confess everything, if only to take away the pain in his eyes and the weariness bogging down his shoulders. She cared about him.

And she knew she shouldn't. Especially after her night with Jack.

Which wasn't even his real name. He had not bothered to tell her. What in heaven's glory was she doing? She'd tangled herself up in far more than she knew what to make sense of. It wasn't like her to be so careless.

"I need your help again," Claude said with a weary sigh. "With the victims. Well, with one victim, as the other was a cleaner death."

"Oh." She glanced down at the coffee canister she'd set aside, disappointment rolling through her stomach before she managed to stop it. "I suppose the coffee was a bribe."

Half his mouth twitched in an almost-smile. "My superiors won't pay a female doctor, so I'm taking it upon myself to reimburse you with your favorite drink."

"All you had to do was bribe me with the macabre and good company."

"Oh?" He lifted an eyebrow, and for a moment, the darkness and exhaustion disappeared from his countenance. "I had no idea you thought so highly of me."

She playfully smacked his shoulder, which elicited a tired smile from his lips. "I was talking about the corpses. They're delightful company, so I hear."

By the stars, she had to stop flirting and end whatever this was. She'd made her choice.

She cleared her throat and reached for her basket to pack supplies. But too late, she realized it was the same basket she hadn't touched since her visit to Claude's office. The same basket where she had hidden his case files. The same basket in which they still hid.

And too late, she was unable to correct herself as the basket tipped off balance with the odd distribution of weight, and the files spilled out of the basket and fluttered to the floor.

All over Claude's feet.

They both stared at the files, shock in each of their expressions. And then he slowly lifted his gaze, his eyes searching hers as if looking for innocence he was not going to find.

"I-I-I'm sorry," she stammered, the words inadequate on her tongue. She was sorry for so many things, but by now the list had grown too long to conceal.

"You were the one who took my files," he accused in a disbelieving, husky tone. "I've spent weeks on this case. Months! And here you were buttering me up so I would never suspect you."

She ran her hands over her hair and locked her fingers behind her neck as the stress of the entire situation came tumbling down like a pile of boulders crashing down a mountain. "It's not what it looks like, Claude. I swear!"

"Not what it looks like?" he said, raising his voice as he gestured to the loose papers scattered over the floor. "It was you! You lied. You…you…*kissed* me! It all makes sense now, and it makes me sick to my stomach."

One of her patients stuck his head out of the curtain concealing him, unabashedly watching their argument unfold.

She dropped her hands to her side and spun to face him, ignoring the several pairs of eyes watching them. She was eighty percent sure one of them was Norma hiding behind the corner. "This case is a very bad idea. I've been telling you this for weeks."

"That's not for you to decide. This is my occupation, Clara. This is my *livelihood*. Besides, what gives you the right to do something like this?"

"You don't know what you're mixed up in!"

"And you do?"

She clamped her mouth shut, but her silence was enough to incriminate her. His jaw became slack. His eyes stared back at her in disbelief. The weight of the hurt and betrayal in his expression was enough to nearly crumple her.

"What do you know?" He grabbed her wrist and held on tight, leading her away from watchful eyes and listening ears, stopping only when they reached the middle of the hallway. When she tried to pull away, his grip only tightened. "Tell me what you know. Are you involved? Who did you steal the files for? Are you the Ripper's accomplice?"

"At least bribe me with a night on the town before throwing all your questions at me," she jested feebly, her stomach on the verge of heaving. This was not what she'd wanted. Surely, she was going to jail. And for what? Had Jack used her? Showered her with kisses and sweet words until she was head over heels and committed to him? She had helped him slow down the detective's case, and she would be the one to pay for it.

Although she still didn't want to betray the Ripper despite everything, she had to give Claude something. Anything. Even a portion of the truth.

"I had to pick up a shipment from the post office at night," she said in a shaky tone. "I-I-I was followed by vampires. They tried to infect me with…with…"

She squeezed her eyes shut, and only then did Claude's grip on her relax. However, he didn't release her.

"With what?" he asked softly, the hardness in his eyes melting to something kinder and more human. "And you should have told me. You knew you could trust me with this. I'm trying to help."

Shaking her head, she took a step back, and this time, he allowed her to take her wrist back. "This is bigger than you, Claude. You'll get yourself killed, and I can't stand the thought of you getting hurt."

A storm of emotion erupted in the blue of his eyes. Betrayal. Passion. A spark of determination. "What are you infected with? Vampirism?"

She pressed her lips together and stared at the floor rather than the tempest in his eyes. "I'm not infected with anything. I was saved from the vampires before they managed to do anything."

"Saved by whom?" Then he gasped, and she glanced up to find his eyes widening. "The Ripper. And now you're in his debt."

Even the smallest bits of information clearly allowed him to connect the strings between his unknowns. He was too intelligent. No wonder Jack didn't want her to tell him anything.

"I am not indebted to anyone."

"I don't believe that. You are too smart to help a killer."

"He's not a killer. It's not what you think, Claude."

He gripped either of her shoulders and squeezed gently. "Then tell me what it is. Tell me so I might understand." When she didn't answer, he gave her a desperate, pleading look. "What sort of creature is he?"

Clara was torn between telling Claude everything and keeping silent. No matter what she did, it would put either him or Jack in danger. What was the right thing to do? Who could she trust?

"How long have you been involved?" he asked when her mouth remained closed. But this time, the tips of his fingers brushed tenderly against her cheek. She couldn't stand it. She enjoyed the tender touch far too much. However, she'd made her choice.

Claude sighed and dropped his hand in her silence. "I'll give you a couple hours to get your story straight. Because...because I care about you. But I can't ignore this. Not even for you. I'll bring the police by, some of *my* colleagues, and we'll question you then."

"Why do you like me?" she blurted, her gaze darting from the coffee canister to the hand he'd touched her with so gently to his crazed yet passionate expression.

"I don't know!" He clutched his head, his eyes wild. "I mean, I do know. But I feel something deeper that shouldn't be there. Something I don't remember. Like a dream I cannot recall when I wake." He spun to face her. "But what I do know is that when I look at you…" He swallowed. "When I look at you, Clara, I want to stay by your side. I want to protect you."

She pointed an accusatory finger at his chest. "This is not protecting me. You are turning me in for the crime of keeping you safe."

"You stole evidence for my case. No, you stole my case entirely! And two people died because of it."

"Don't pin their deaths on me. All I did was hinder your investigation."

"To stall me. Why?"

"I'm not sure." She closed her eyes and rubbed a finger over the bridge of her nose. "I don't know, Claude. I know I'm foolish for trusting blindly, but I believe this is the right thing to do."

"How is this possibly the right thing to do? You are working against me."

The ache in her head only seemed to grow. "What am I supposed to do? Allow you to walk into a den of vampires on your own?"

He swore under his breath. "There is an entire den here? By the holy shadows of our maker, what am I up against? I wasn't even supposed to be hunting vampires."

"You cannot hunt him!" she rasped, clinging onto his arms in desperation. "He's innocent. I swear."

"Then it wasn't the Ripper tearing apart these women?"

She squeezed her eyes shut and hung her head. No matter what she said, it would vilify the Ripper. And to say anything more might tip Claude off that Jack was a ghoul, which would give him an idea of how to hunt him.

What could she possibly say that wouldn't hurt Jack?

Therefore, she said nothing.

"Your silence is all the answer I need," he murmured, extracting his arms from beneath her hands. "I'm sorry, Clara. I need more information to prevent further deaths. I never wished for you to get caught in the crossfire." He started down the hallway but stopped for a moment without turning to face her. "I will return soon with my team. If you will not give me anything, then we will need to conduct a thorough search of your home."

She balled her hands into fists, her arms shaking at the thought of anything bad happening to Jack. "If you kill him, I will never forgive you."

He hung his head, remaining in the hallway for several beats of silence before continuing on his way and exiting the estate. She had to warn Jack. But how? She only ever saw him at night, which was still several hours away.

But still, she waited, hardly able to pay attention to her patients as she bit her nails, pulled out her pocket watch every five minutes, and glanced toward the window to wait for darkness to fall over Whitechapel.

And finally, it did. But neither Claude nor Jack returned to the estate. At least not yet.

A knock sounded on the front door, spiking her pulse to her neck. Jack wouldn't have knocked. It was Claude to come search the house. Instinct told her to conceal any traces of Jack, but no matter what she attempted to hide, she was certain Claude could find it. Her *involvement* with the ghoul would be exposed, surely. There was nothing she could do but watch as her secrets unraveled to his observant eye.

She wiped her sweaty palms on her apron, her heart racing as she strode down the hallway and stood in front of the door without opening it. Someone knocked a second time, and she knew she couldn't ignore it. Claude usually walked right in. He was offering her more time, more warning. It was all he seemed willing to give.

Taking a deep breath, she reached for the door handle and turned.

However, when she opened the door, it wasn't Claude and his team on the other side but the regular police on her doorstep.

And each wore grim expressions.

The room spun around her. Her mind buzzed with dizziness. For a moment, she could hear nothing other than the roaring in her veins and the pulse in her ears. A chill climbed over her spine, down her arms, and to the very tips of her fingers.

No, no, no. Please, no.

"I'm sorry," one of the officers said as he took off his hat and held it to his chest. "Your sister... Mazie..."

Her head spun. Breaths became shallow and rapid. Nothing could have affected her so much. Not blood, death, or the macabre. But the thought of anything terrible happening to her sisters was enough for her to lose all sense of control.

The world spun, and the last thing she saw with clarity was the officer's look of regret on his face before she tipped precariously to the side and her surroundings turned dark.

Chapter Twelve

An officer fanned Clara's face from where she sat within the arms of a cushioned chair, her mind still spinning as she tried to listen to another officer's report. With her mind spinning and her heart pulsing through her ears, she only caught bits and pieces of the situation.

But it was enough.

Mazie had escaped outside to get fresh air during her break at the Ten Bells Pub. Or that was one account from a patron, drunk at that. Another testimony claimed she'd left with someone, lured outside by a handsome stranger.

When her sister had been absent for too long, the owner had gone out looking for her, only to find splotches of fresh blood and a scene in the alleyway that appeared to be none other than a scuffle.

Now, Mazie was missing. Presumed dead. But Clara's disbelieving heart refused to acknowledge their presumptions in the slightest. Mazie may be stupid sometimes, but she wasn't entirely lacking wits.

"She's missing," the officer with the thin, curled mustache repeated for the second time. "And based on all the blood at the scene... She's presumed dead."

"There is no body," Clara argued, defiance burning in her eyes.

"No, but—"

"If there is no body, you cannot prove her death." Until she saw her sister's lifeless corpse with her own eyes, she refused to believe she was gone. "Was anything left at the scene?"

The officer grimaced. "Nothing a lady should hear about."

She stood on surprisingly sturdy feet and poked the man repeatedly in the chest. "I have seen things that would make a grown man cry. Tell me what you found."

Again, he grimaced as he glanced over his shoulder. When another officer nodded his permission, he said, "A torn scarf, a bloodied glove, and..."

"And?"

"And, well, something that appears to be a canine tooth. It's currently in evidence to figure out what we're dealing with."

A canine tooth...

Suddenly, all the blood rushed from her face when she realized what a sharp, elongated tooth might mean.

Vampire.

Mazie was taken by vampires. It was the only logical solution. Had they infected her? What would happen if they had?

She was going to be sick.

Another realization hit her, and she covered her mouth with her hand when she truly thought she might retch. In the alleyway, the vampires had tried to infect her. Jack had come to her rescue. If they wanted Jack, they were getting to him by getting to Clara. Or perhaps they were angry that she'd gotten away in the first place.

And like the foolish woman she was, she began hatching a plan. A terrible plan. A plan that could get herself killed or worse.

But it was the only plan she had, and if she didn't start to enact it quickly, she might never see Mazie again as she once was.

She snatched a piece of parchment and a quill from the table near the door and wrote as neatly as her racing heart allowed. In reality, she worried the warning note was illegible as it was.

i should have Gone and told you everytHing when yOu were here. don't let this detract yoU from your originaL goal.
-Clara

The capitalized letters spelled *GHOUL*. It was all she could do without tipping off anyone else, such as the ignorant officers, and placing them in danger as well. Claude would know what it meant.

She couldn't wait around for Jack to show his face. Nor could she scour the city trying to find Claude. If there was any chance to help her sister, this was it. Claude was going to have to find *her*.

And if he couldn't or wouldn't…

Well, then she was on her own.

But Claude said she could trust him. And right now? She was choosing to do so. If he could hunt down Jack, they would have a chance to save Mazie. If she was still alive.

She folded up the note, placed it in an envelope, and handed it to the mustached officer. "If you see Detective La Cour, please give it to him immediately." She paused and stared blankly at the floor. "I want to be alone."

The man dipped his head and placed his hat back on. "I'm very sorry, Miss Thompson. If anything turns up, we'll let you know."

The officers turned to leave, and she watched them as they exited the estate. The moment the door closed behind them, Clara rushed back toward the infirmary and began snatching a few supplies and stuffing them into her pocket. A rolled bandage. Needle and catgut thread. Two scalpels.

But a sniff from the corner urged her to spin around to find Norma dabbing at her eyes with a handkerchief. Although her sister said nothing, she had clearly overheard her conversation with the police.

"Be strong," Clara murmured, squeezing Norma's shoulders and pulling her into an embrace. She stroked her sister's long, golden curls kinked around her shoulders as if she'd recently pulled pins out of her hair. "We'll find Mazie, and she will be just fine."

Norma shook her head, her fingers trembling as she swiped the tears running down her cheeks with her handkerchief. "I heard what the officers said."

She lifted Norma's chin until she met her gaze. "You listen to *me*. Not to them. A death is never confirmed without a body. Mazie is a fighter. If anyone could have survived, it's her. I refuse to believe she's gone. She's too stubborn for that."

Watery laughter escaped Norma's mouth. "I suppose you're right. There is no sense in mourning just yet."

Clara squeezed her sister's shoulders reassuringly and lied to her face, because sometimes lies were necessary. "The police will find her. Don't you worry about a thing. Go off to bed, and don't leave the house. Don't let anyone in, either. No visitors. No patients. No one."

Norma swiped the back of her hand across her teary eyes. "What about you? You never turn down a patient."

"I won't be able to rest without knowing you are safe. Promise me, Norma."

Norma nodded and untied her apron from around her waist, tossing it into the dirty hamper resting against the wall. She started toward the hallway but paused mid-step and glanced over her shoulder.

"Your friend will help, won't he?"

"My friend?" Admittedly, she had few friends and wasn't sure what she meant. "Yes, I'm sure the detective will make this a priority."

But Norma shook her head. "Your other friend."

The blood drained from Clara's face when she realized what her sister referred to. The Ripper. "How do you know about him?"

"He's come by several times. He scared me at first. But he was kind. He's misunderstood but means no harm."

Clara sagged against the wall as unexpected relief lifted a portion of the weight pressing down on her shoulders. Perhaps she wasn't as insane as she'd previously thought. If Norma thought well of Jack, then she knew she hadn't misjudged his character.

"He's a good man." Even though she didn't know his name. Even though she had never seen him in broad daylight. But she trusted her gut instinct, which told her she could place her trust in him.

With a nod, Norma continued on her way down the hallway, and Clara kept still until she caught the quiet patter of her feet on the staircase. Only then did she move quickly to snatch several more items from the infirmary, don on a coat, and slip outside to the back of the house to try to avoid notice by anyone who might still linger outside or be watching from a window.

She slowly and quietly rounded the estate, her heart beating fiercely in her chest. The loud pulse in her ears seemed to shout Mazie's name with each beat.

Although she had no idea where the den of vampires resided, she did know one thing—a trail always started somewhere.

The skies burned like fire above her, with yellow, red, and orange hues to match the turmoil running rampant through her soul. As she followed the roads through Whitechapel, those sunset colors slowly faded into a darker hue until only a faint pink lingered in the sky.

The crowds thickened the nearer she approached the Ten Bells. The hum of murmuring voices grew into a loud roar when she rounded the corner and lost herself in the throng of people surrounding the pub.

Clara stood on her toes and craned her neck to try to peer over the shoulders of a woman several centimeters taller than her, but an even taller man blocked her line of sight. For just a moment, the crowd shifted to give her a better look at the crime scene.

Police officers kept the crowd at bay with their bodies when the rope seemed to have little effect at holding them back.

She craned her neck again in search of a certain blond-haired detective, but as far as she could see, Claude was absent from the scene.

If not here, then where was he?

No time remained to ponder over his whereabouts when she had a sister to find.

Lampposts flickered to life as the lamplighters quietly went about their jobs, racing against the waning light. Shadows seemed to follow in her wake as she pulled away from the throng and moved closer to the partitioned-off alleyway behind the pub. Dark alleyways appeared to be a vampire favorite, and it was as good of a start as any.

Other nosey passersby tried to cross the rope line for a better look at the crime scene, which occupied two officers' attention long enough for them to step away from the alley. Clara glanced back and forth, took a deep breath to steel her nerves, and slipped beneath the rope and between the thin brick walls casting heavy shadows at her feet like a lure to catch a prized fish.

Someone called after her. She didn't turn to look and instead quickened her pace around full garbage bins and empty crates.

Until the darkness swallowed her whole.

She carried no lantern, no candle, could not use the sunlight for direction. But it didn't matter. Finding her way was not her ultimate goal.

Because the vampires were going to come to her.

The voices beside the pub faded in the distance until they were only a dull trickle in comparison to a roaring waterfall of noise. She paused to listen to her surroundings. An incoherent mumbling coming from a homeless man somewhere around the corner. A drip of water running down the rooftop behind her. The clomping of hooves from a passing carriage the next street over.

Otherwise, all was quiet. She was alone.

Determination stole over her as she pulled out the scalpel from her pocket, and not giving herself a moment to reflect on her decision, she slit the small blade across her palm.

She hissed at the sting of pain and watched as a rivulet of blood dripped down her hand. It pooled at the tip of her finger and plummeted toward the ground. But before it plopped onto the cobblestone, someone caught her hand and brought it smoothly and silently to their mouth, licking the blood from her palm.

"I was waiting for you," the man whispered in her ear in a seductive tone.

She squeezed her eyes shut and released a shuddering breath. Although every instinct in her body screamed at her to run, to fight, to flee, she remained still and accepted the fate she had brought onto herself.

"Where is my sister?" she asked in a hoarse voice.

"Exactly where you think she is."

In the den of vampires, then.

"Bring me to her."

The vampire playfully nipped at her ear. "As you wish, my dear." He draped a silk handkerchief over her eyes and tied it behind her head, effectively blinding her senses. "But as some people say... Be careful what you wish for."

Then he picked her up in a quick, agile swoop, and she allowed herself to be captured by the very creature that had created chaos all across Whitechapel.

And she didn't know if she would make it back out alive.

Chapter Thirteen

ank water and musty walls greeted her senses first, followed by the squeal of a metal door and then a resounding *bang* as it slammed shut behind them. Whispering voices echoed on either side of her as the vampire dragged her forward by hands bound by scratchy rope. A blindfold continued to cover her eyes, but if they'd been open, she was sure she would find an eerie darkness awaiting her on the other side of the velvety fabric.

A couple hisses bounced off what sounded like brick ceilings. Flutters of air passed her, and the small hairs on her arms raised when she sensed what could only be predators. Smelling her. Tasting the very air she breathed.

Vampires.

Claude had only mentioned vampires briefly during their conversation. Aside from what she'd learned from books and terrifying stories meant to scare children into obedience, she had no idea what they were really like.

And she didn't want to.

Unfortunately, she had no choice now.

A touch as brief as the kiss of a breeze guided her forward until the slapping water against her shoes transitioned into something soft and mushy that stank like damp carpet. Another vampire hissed as she passed. The brush of a cold hand against her throat caused her to jump and stifle a scream. But the possessive caress ended with a growl behind her, the feeling of a gust of wind near her face, and then a whimper in front of her as if someone had gotten punched. Or scratched. She wasn't sure.

The air turned chillier, enough for her to long to rub her hands up and down her arms to gather warmth to her body, but her wrists were bound together, restricting her movements.

A light touch on the small of her back guided her forward, and her arm brushed against something that felt like a cold metal rod. Finally, someone tugged at her bindings and freed her hands, followed by the light pull of the velvety handkerchief around her eyes.

The handkerchief fell free, and she blinked several times to adjust to the darkness caving in on all sides. She stood within a large cage in the middle of the room, dank stone walls surrounding her. One exit lay in front of her, along with another behind, one she assumed she had entered through judging by how many vampires gathered near it.

She released a startled gasp as a woman appeared suddenly in front of her, not a single brunette strand of her hair out of place in the bun piled atop her head. Her quick, airy touch searched her body, so light that Clara hardly felt the pressure at all.

And then the woman's body evaporated into mist, reappearing on the opposite end of the bars moments before the cage door squealed shut, and another vampire turned the lock with a key.

The woman who had searched her dipped her head. "Lord Ferdinand," she said, addressing the leader, "she has scalpels and a needle in her pocket."

"Are they made of silver?"

"Well, no."

"Then let her keep them if it gives her a false sense of safety."

Clara rushed toward the bars and gripped them tightly with desperation burning in each finger. "What about my sister? You promised to take me to Mazie."

The vampire chuckled, his fangs almost glowing in the dim light of the prison. "And I have. But the question you must ask yourself... Does she want to leave?"

A shuddering breath escaped her lips as her gaze darted from silhouette to silhouette, trying in vain to find one that might belong to Mazie. "You have me. Now I demand that you release her."

Again, he laughed, his eyes flashing red with thirst. "She was never my prisoner. But you, on the other hand... There is always an exception for you."

"You promised you wouldn't hurt her," a small voice said on the opposite side of the room.

Clara squinted her eyes as if the simple action might allow her to see better in the darkness. But all she found was a feminine silhouette illuminated by a torch flickering its light behind her.

Dread fell to the very pits of her stomach. Her fingers stiffened around the bars in a similar way her neck refused to turn, and her eyes were unable to blink. "Mazie?" she croaked.

The male vampire answered, "And I haven't hurt her, dear Mazie. I only want her ghoul. I promise she will come to no harm."

Shaking her head, Clara continued to stare at the woman in disbelief. Her mind whirred quickly, unable to stop long enough for her to make sense of the situation.

But then the figure took several slow steps forward, entering the aura of light emanating from the torches on either side of the room. Mazie's long blonde hair tumbled in waves down her back. Her thin eyebrows were furrowed, her gaze glued to the ground. And then she glanced up.

Clara's heart skidded to a stop, ice slowly crawling across the tough, warm membrane.

Mazie's eyes were red.

"What have they done to you?" she whispered, but the small sound echoed off the walls, nonetheless.

When her sister didn't answer immediately, Ferdinand flicked his wrist, and many of the others disappeared from the room as quickly as a light snuffing out, leaving behind nothing but wisps of smoke. Only a few remained.

Finally, Mazie answered, "Only what I've asked them to do. Once this business with Whitechapel is done, we are relocating somewhere better. Nicer." She paused, biting her lip hesitantly with the tip of a single elongated fang. "You could come with us."

"These are vampires, Mazie!" Clara hissed, glancing cautiously between each creature. "You don't know what you're doing. You don't know what you're risking."

Mazie balled her hands into fists, her arms shaking. "We were going to lose the house."

She blinked several times to try to make sense of her sister's words. "What are you talking about? I've kept the finances under control."

But her sister shook her head profusely. "The lender came by while you were gone several years ago. He said that after Papa's death, he had shown us mercy by putting off collecting property expenses. He threatened to make us back pay for previous years of unpaid expenses. Or I could work for him, and he needn't bother needling you for money."

The defeated look on her face told her what this work was without even opening her mouth.

Clara sagged against the bars, her head drooping. "You could have come to me. You *should* have come to me. I could have dealt with this."

Out of the corner of her eye, she noticed Mazie shaking her head. "You think I don't see what you do. You think I don't help. I couldn't burden you with this. I knew how upset it would make you."

"But…" She wasn't sure what she could say. Not after this terrible confession. "How long have you been…" She lifted her head and gestured to all of Mazie. "…this?"

Mazie hissed and flashed her pointed fangs. "You took away my one chance at escaping that terrible life, Clara. You stole Claude's affections. I had to figure out something else. Because I couldn't stand… I couldn't do it anymore." She gestured to the male vampire. "Ferdinand found me. He turned me at my own request, and I am no longer forced to lie on my back for strangers."

Squeezing her eyes shut, Clara made no attempt to bat away the guilt climbing over her body like thorny vines. Even after everything she'd done to shelter her sisters, the harsh world had found them, anyway. She could not save them. And now? She had needlessly put Jack in danger by allowing herself to get captured. She could not save anyone. All she managed to do was bring more harm upon the people she cared for.

Physicians vowed to help, not hinder. But if she couldn't even help her own family?

What did that make her?

Useless.

The vampires turned to leave, and in a desperate attempt to keep Mazie with her longer, she said, "All the stories I've heard of vampires are that they love to live up their lavish lifestyles. If I didn't know better, I'd say we're in a sewer."

Ferdinand snorted. "In Whitechapel? The only people living lavish lifestyles are those who cast too large of a shadow that they can't see the people beneath. This city deserves what's coming to them. Now, if your ghoul would only show up, we can finally begin this in earnest."

"Why?" she croaked when it felt as if her throat were clogged with impenetrable mucus. "Why are you doing this?"

"To give us the life we deserve. When the city is in chaos, when those people casting large shadows are dealt with permanently, we can intercede. Take advantage of that chaos. Climb our way to the top when there is no one to interfere." He shared a small smile with Mazie. "First Whitechapel. Then London. We'll be an unstoppable force."

"And what of the rabid ghouls running amuck?"

Ferdinand chuckled. "How did you think we'll rise to the top? By saving the city from our own creations." He held his hand out in front of him and inspected his nails. "Unfortunately, there will be plenty of casualties. But change never happens without a little bloodshed."

Clara shook her head with disbelief and glanced at her sister. "You can't possibly go along with this, Mazie."

A flash of red eyes accompanied her sister's blatant anger, her jaw snapping down to show off her fangs. "Anything is better than what I have endured. I don't care what it takes. I'm not lying on my back any longer."

She sagged further against the bars in absolute defeat. "Forgive me. You never should have had to endure such a fate."

The defiance and caution momentarily melted from Mazie's countenance, but her defensive walls quickly returned as she turned on her heel with a huff. "I'm sorry it had to come to this. If there had been any other way…"

Mazie's words trailed off, leaving the smallest bit of room for… For what? Familial connection? Because that had been absent for years, it seemed.

"Don't hurt my ghoul," she begged instead. "He…he's important to me."

A malicious smile turned up on Ferdinand's lips as he looped his arm through Mazie's. "We are counting on that."

Together, they disappeared from the room, and not once did her sister glance back before even her silhouette vanished from the dim torch light. She continued to reel with disbelief long after, trying to make sense of what had happened. Of what was about to happen.

Silently, she begged Jack to stay away. If Ferdinand had promised she would come to no harm, then the only person in danger was her ghoul. At least for now. And only if he kept his promise. She needed to find a way to escape before Jack put himself in harm's way for her sake.

She removed the items in her pocket and set them side by side on the ground in front of her. Two scalpels. A bandage. Needle and thread. Nothing silver. No garlic. No holy water or silver cross. If those were truly a vampire's weakness.

"Mazie," she whispered, her shoulders slumping with defeat. "What have you done?"

And worst of all...

Clara had unknowingly pushed her sister toward this fate. Perhaps *she* was the one to blame.

Drip. Drip. Sleep. *Drip. Drip.* Sleep.

Her routine consisted of listening to the echo of droplets of water splashing into a puddle somewhere in the corner of the room and fighting off the fatigue of a long night. She kept thinking she heard footsteps, and perhaps a couple of times she swore a pair of eyes blinked in the darkness.

But after some time, she convinced herself it was her own mind playing tricks on her.

Or perhaps not...

A pair of red dots blinked in the darkness, and Clara squinted to try to find the outline of someone's profile, only to find nothing of note. It was unnerving to feel like someone might be watching her but not being able to see them clearly.

A shiver raked down her body as the chill of her surroundings seeped into her being. She tugged her sleeves farther over her wrists and even attempted to use her thin apron as a blanket, but nothing managed to push away the fierce chill growing colder by the moment. If this was where the vampires lived, she didn't blame them for wanting something better.

What she *did* find fault with was their means of acquiring such a lavish lifestyle. Hundreds—perhaps even thousands—of people would die to achieve the perfect living conditions in this terrible economy.

Please stay away, she silently begged her ghoul. If the vampires got hold of his blood, no one would be safe.

But even as she prayed in her mind that he might keep his distance, she knew. She *knew* he would not stay away while his mate was in danger in the center of a den of vampires. He would come for her, and she would not be able to forgive herself when he did.

What felt like only minutes later, Clara jolted awake when a fierce roar echoed down the stone hallway and into the prison. She shot upright and took the metal bars in a tight grip while intently watching the doorway.

She recognized that growl. She'd heard it before when Jack had protected her from the vampires in the city.

Shouts, cries, and roars reached her ears, followed by the deafening crash of splintering wood and breaking bricks. Vampires screamed. Others hissed, followed by cries of surprise or pain.

Another angered roar shook her prison, and she launched onto shaky feet when it grew closer, louder. She tugged and prodded on the bars keeping her captive. When her efforts proved in vain, she snatched one of her scalpels from the ground and shoved the sharp end into the keyhole. Although she knew nothing about picking locks, she pushed and jiggled without success.

When the lock refused to give, she braced one of her feet against the bars, her skirt riding up her leg until her stockings and underskirts were exposed. Then, she tugged on the door with all her might until her muscles protested the harsh strain and her elbows threatened to pop out of their sockets.

She needed to get out of here. She wasn't about to become a placid duck waiting to get wringed and plucked.

She tugged hard again, but only the bottom of the door gave way while the rest remained shut as if welded together by strong iron.

And then the atmosphere turned quiet.

Clara's head shot up, her eyes wide with panic as her gaze darted toward the door. The sound of something large being dragged permeated the eerie quiet. At least until a large mass of muscle, spikes, and ragged clothes turned around the corner...

...with two vampires dragging him like a lifeless corpse.

"Jack!" she shrieked, abandoning her efforts at the door to dart across the prison and cling onto the bars closest to him.

The vampires dragged his limp body toward the same cell, and in a quick movement, they unlocked the door, threw him inside, and locked the door behind them.

"If he touches those bars," one of the vampires warned, a gash in his face seeping blood from cheekbone to cheekbone, "the metal is poison to him. It will kill him."

Clara glared fiercely at the retreating vampires, her breaths coming fast and labored, filled with anger and hatred. But when Jack groaned, and his head shifted to the side, her attention turned entirely to him.

"Jack!" She rushed toward him and skidded to her knees at his side.

Another vampire she hadn't noticed hissed and spit a yellowish liquid at the Ripper's feet she could only assume was venom, because it looked like no saliva she was familiar with. In the man's hand was a vial filled with a black substance.

Ghoul's blood.

No, no, no!

"You shouldn't have come!" she cried and, without hesitation, grabbed his hands and held on tight. The familiar sharp angles of his face and the deep color of his skin felt like a comforting glove slipping over her heart. She'd always felt safe with him. That had never changed. "They have your blood. Whitechapel is in danger."

After the vampires spoke in low tones to one another, they left the room as if they had pressing matters to attend to now that they had the blood they needed.

"*You* were in danger!" he replied in a slurred tone. "I don't care about the rest of the city when you are the one I cannot live without."

"I thought you were supposed to be a hero," she jested, tears of both hurt and relief falling down her cheeks as she lightly stroked his face.

"Beasts are never heroes. They are the ones everybody wants to call a villain."

"You are *my* hero then," she whispered.

"I couldn't save you."

"You came after me when no one else would. For years, I have been healing and saving lives, and not one of those people would care to do the same for me. But you did."

He grunted and tried to sit, though she wasn't sure if it was because he was in pain or if he had nothing to say on the matter.

Clara noticed the blood coating Jack's abdomen, where he must have ripped open his stitches, and the discoloration of his skin. But what drew her gaze was the sheen of black dripping from his head and trailing down his neck. She gasped, her fingers fluttering over the wound. "Jack, you're injured."

When she reached for his head, he winced. "My name is not Jack. I should have told you long ago. But it was dangerous."

His words became slurred, and his body unbalanced. As he tipped heavily to one side, she caught him and helped lay him on the ground, away from the bars of the cage that might injure him. The head wound looked bad, but without getting a closer look, she wasn't sure just *how* bad.

She reached for his head again, but he lightly batted her hand away.

"Jack," she murmured quietly, glancing around her to make sure they were still alone. "You need medical attention. I can help."

He shook his head and hissed through his sharp teeth. "You need the truth." He winced again. "But first, we need to get you out of here. You need to stand directly beneath sunlight. That way, the vampires can't touch you."

"And you?" she asked, her voice breaking. "You think I will leave you at the vampires' mercy? And Mazie? I don't care what happens to me as long as she is safe."

"*I* care about what happens to you!" he thundered, but the outburst caused him to tip again as if losing consciousness. If he lost any more blood, he would certainly keel over soon. The next words from his mouth were so slurred that she hardly made sense of them. "You are my mate. *I* care about what happens to you. And I could not stand idle while you were in danger. I love you."

Her eyes widened, and her hand flew to her heart. For several long beats, she stared back at him in disbelief, wondering if she'd misheard his confession when he was only half-conscious.

But no. He looked at her with enough clarity in his yellow eyes for her to know the truth. He'd meant those words. He loved her.

"Jack," she whispered.

Weakly, his hand grasped hers and squeezed with very little strength. "That is not my name. Forgive me, Clara. I never wanted to deceive you like this."

She opened her mouth to ask after his meaning, but then the faintest sliver of sunlight entered through the barred windows near the ceiling, officially ending the terrors of the night and pulling her into a brand-new day.

The stream of sunlight touched her shoulder like the faintest hope in a vat of darkness. A torturous hope. Because even as she reached out to touch its thin warmth, she could not grasp it within her hands. It wasn't enough sunlight to defeat one vampire, let alone an entire den.

She turned back to Jack. Her heart leaped to her throat when his large mass was missing as if he'd dissolved into the sunlight himself.

But then she noticed the smaller heap in his place. That person groaned and shifted, and her nursing instincts reared its head as she scrambled toward the man on her hands and knees. She grabbed his partially bare shoulder and turned him from his stomach to his back.

A hiss of shock escaped her as if the mere contact with him burned her hand. She recognized the man's tall, intimidating frame. His angular face. The demon's kiss striking a scar through his mouth. And as he blearily opened his eyes, she knew the intense blue staring back at her, as she'd seen it many times.

Despite the dirt coating the blond of his hair and the usual elegant swoop in a mess of dirty strands, she knew him. Without a doubt.

He was the detective apparently trying to solve his own case.

Claude La Cour.

Chapter Fourteen

lara knelt back on her heels and stared at Claude with disbelief burning in her eyes. Disbelief. Shame. Anger. Shock. All this time, both Jack and Claude had been pursuing her. And all this time, they had been the same person.

However, it seemed as if she was the only one in their little trio who hadn't known. She'd been played the fool. Pining after the handsome detective and longing for the creature of the night.

How much was the truth?

How much was a lie?

And if Jack the Ripper and Detective La Cour were the same person… Was he simply putting up appearances and telling lies to keep the police off his tail? Quite literally? Or was something more sinister going on?

"Ugh," he groaned as he tried to sit with great effort, clutching his face with one hand as if it pained him. One *human* hand. He was no longer a ghoul. For now. "My head hurts."

"Shh," she cautioned as she placed a hand on his chest and gently pushed him back into a supine position. Every pore in her body wanted to scream at him, to demand answers. But he was injured. Yelling and arguing might only make things worse. "Try not to move until I assess that head injury."

"Clara?" His eyes fluttered open, but his stare remained unfocused as he tried but failed to maintain eye contact. "What are you doing here? Where are we…"

He trailed off, blinking heavily as he scanned their surroundings. After a moment, he swore and tried to sit up again, but he quickly collapsed into her shoulder when he couldn't keep himself upright. Still, he stuck out an arm as if to shield her from…from what, exactly?

"Stay still, I said," she growled as she turned his head to the side to inspect his wound. The side of his head bled profusely. He'd hit it hard. Or perhaps someone had bashed it in. "And while you're at it," she said in an accusatory tone when she just couldn't help herself, "bring back Jack. We'll need him."

"Jack?" he slurred, reaching out to her but missing several times until his hand brushed against her knee. "Clara, this looks like a vampire den. We have to escape."

Clara sat up straighter and stared at him with wide eyes. Shock coursed through her the moment she made the realization, the very instant she connected the missing pieces of the intricate puzzle together.

Claude La Cour didn't know he was Jack the Ripper.

No, no, no. She must be mistaken! Either she'd hit her head, and it had been Claude the entire time in the prison with her, or somehow, Jack and Claude had traded places. They couldn't possibly be the same person. It made no sense for him to have no memory of a beastly transformation.

Or Claude could be lying...

The thought struck her and clung on tight, refusing to abate. She desperately wanted to believe she hadn't been played the fool, that she hadn't been so desperate for love that she'd allowed herself to get sucked into a lie. The evidence lay in front of her. The mystery had unraveled. And now she would make him answer for it.

She pointed a menacing finger in his face, her nostrils flaring. "Do you take me for a fool, detective? What game are you playing?"

Claude leaned up on his elbow but groaned and quickly squeezed his eyes shut. "What game am I playing?" he finally gasped, his brows furrowed with pain. "I should ask you the same question. I got your warning and then saw you outside The Ten Bells. You were...panicked. And then I realized why. I called after you. I followed you, tried to keep you from following danger."

"And then what happened?" she hissed, her gaze raking up and down his long form.

His opposite hand pinched the bridge of his nose as if trying to ward off an ache gathered there. "And then I woke up here." He dropped his hand and leveled her with a weary, bloodshot stare. "I don't remember getting clubbed on the back of the head, but that's the only explanation for this." He gestured to their surroundings.

She was unconvinced that was all that happened.

"You're not telling me everything, and you know it. Tell me now, or we're through."

He lifted an eyebrow. "So there's a *we*? Last I was informed, you chose the monster over me."

"You infuriate me! I am infuriated!"

"Hush!" He scanned the room with a careful sweep of his gaze. "We don't want to attract attention."

"It's too late for that." She crossed her arms and leveled him with a waiting stare. "I need to know the truth. What really happened after you followed me?"

Claude sighed and shifted, wincing again after the action seemed to pain him. "I suppose I have not been completely forthright." He dragged a finger along the scar that struck through one side of his mouth and out the other. His *demon's kiss*. "My line of work is not without its risks. I have never told anyone how I got this, but I suppose you deserve the truth."

Her gaze darted to the scar across his mouth, and her cheeks filled with heat when she remembered what that mouth had felt like against hers, what it had tasted like.

He continued, "I was aiding one of my colleagues with hunting a banshee in Ireland several years back. The assignment was supposed to be easy what with how much information we already had on the creature. But..." His gaze appeared far away as if he were someplace other than the prison cage. "Things went sideways. My colleague was killed, and I was left fighting for my life. This scar..." He ran a finger over his mouth again. "It's from a ghoul, a sort of pet the banshee liked to keep."

"What happened?" she whispered, enraptured with his tale.

"I only remember bits and pieces of that fateful night. The vampire. The banshee. My bleeding face. The leg they shattered when I attempted to escape. I hardly remember a thing. Therefore, when I showed up at the office in Paris, everyone was astounded to see me. I wasn't sure how I got there, only that I did."

Clara thought back on what she'd only recently discovered about the Ripper. The story matched. Perhaps he was not lying after all.

But instead of giving him the benefit of her testimony, she waited.

With a sigh, he ran a hand over his face and managed to push himself into a straighter sitting position. "Since then, I cannot remember anything past sundown. I am only lucid at sunrise. This explains why I can't remember how I got here. I assume the vampires must have caught me in my unconscious state. Like I said, my line of work is dangerous, and it makes me plenty of enemies."

Oh.

Everything made sense now. Claude. Jack. Why she'd never seen the Ripper at any time other than nighttime. He'd once said that he succumbed to a deep sleep during the day. Perhaps it was because he was no longer himself. Or rather, he was in another form entirely. One unaware of his existence.

Her gaze roamed over Claude to try to find any similarities between the two, and she found them in the shape of his eyes, in the sweep of his hair, in the long stretch of his hands. Did Jack have a *demon's kiss* just like Claude? She couldn't recall when she'd mainly seen him in the darkness or with shadows flickering across his dark form.

"The Ripper—Jack—asked me to steal the files and destroy them," she admitted. "He told me you would understand later after your initial anger." She released a shaky breath. "Now I understand. He was protecting *you.*"

Claude's eyebrows furrowed. "I don't understand. The only explanation is that he was trying to cover up his trail, to make it harder for me to find him."

She released a humorless laugh as she placed her hand on his chest and shook her head. "No, no, no, no, no. Claude, listen to me. *You* were protecting *yourself.* Jack was protecting Claude." Another shaky breath. "During those times when you blackout, you transition into the very thing you hunt. You become a ghoul."

For a long few moments, he stared at her with disbelief, and then the corners of his eyes crinkled with amusement. "Plenty of insane things have happened in my line of work, but I think I'd remember if I transitioned into a ghoul every night. Even werewolves retain the ability to remember their shifts, even if they don't always remember what happened after the fact."

"I *saw* you, Claude," she murmured. "You did not enter this cell as a human."

Now he stared at her, the amusement completely erased from his expression. "I would have remembered."

This time, it sounded as if he were trying to convince himself.

Softly, she traced the outline of his ragged shirt where it lay open to reveal half his chest. The world caved in on them. All sounds seemed to disappear. It was only the two of them. "Don't you remember us?" she asked in hardly a whisper, tracing the skin peeking out beneath his collarbones. "How you visited me time and again at night? How you kissed me?" She swallowed and dared to lift her gaze. "How you made love to me?"

"I..." He cradled her hand in both of his and spoke in a raspy voice. "I don't remember."

"Perhaps not, but..." Taking a deep breath, she soldiered on. "But I think you know. You told me that the moment you saw me, the moment you caught my scent in that alleyway when you saved me from those vampires, you knew I was your mate. And in your human form, you told me you felt a strong urge to protect me, but you weren't entirely sure why."

Again, he squeezed his eyes shut as if the confusion and disorientation was too much to handle. "I just don't remember, Clara. It can't possibly be true." He shook his head in disbelief before he opened his eyes and stared at their hands. "All the people I might have hurt. The people I might have killed... I can't believe it. I don't want to believe it."

She pulled her hand out of his grip, her shoulders slumping with heartache. Sure, she knew Jack loved her. But did it count if only half of him cared?

"You killed those women to prevent the ghoul infection from spreading," she murmured. "*Jack* killed them. He—you— had no choice."

"Infection? What infection?" When she traced the scar over his mouth, his eyes widened with realization. "I was infected all those years ago. *Created.* By that ghoul. That's how... That's why..."

Quirking her mouth to the side, she replied, "I don't know how it works. I only know what you've told me."

He stood suddenly, enough for the blood to likely rush from his head and make him dizzy. He reached out to catch himself on the bars, but she quickly snatched his hand away from the metal and used her own weight to support him.

"Don't touch them," she warned. "A vampire said it would poison a ghoul."

She stood on her tiptoes to survey the damage done to his head, but to her shock, the wound was smaller than it had been only minutes ago. Whatever ghoul tendencies raced through his blood, he healed quickly.

Just to be sure, she took her discarded cloth that lay on the floor and dabbed at his wound. He winced but remained silent through her administration. She should have done this the moment he'd stepped foot in the cell, but she'd been too shocked. Curses! She was a nurse for Pete's sake.

However, very little blood came back on the cloth, especially compared to how much red coated one side of his hair, dried as a drip down his skin, and soaked into the collar of his shirt. Despite being covered in blood and a few bruises, she'd never been more attracted to him. Because now she knew he was her ghoul. Her dear, beloved ghoul.

They would get through this. They *had* to.

"What do we do Claude?" she asked, her shoulders slumping with despairing defeat. "What are we supposed to do?"

He reached for her, and her heart warmed with sudden relief as he threaded his fingers through hers. "This is not my first shot of whiskey," he replied, the intense blue of his eyes boring into her in the most pleasant manner. Yes, his eyes were the same as Jack's, only a different color. How had she not noticed before? "I have an idea."

Chapter Fifteen

As Claude had predicted, the vampires began stirring closer to sundown, judging by the scuffs of shoes against the echoing floor and low, muttering voices. How many vampires lived down here? How many were considered normal for a vampire den?

Claude's hardened expression silently told her that this was a large den, but she didn't dare even whisper her questions, afraid one of the vampires might hear her speak.

Soon enough, the faintest sliver of sunlight peeking into the room dissipated like a flame extinguished by a quiet breath. Sundown had arrived. And with it…

A grunt pulled her attention toward Claude's tall frame. He grunted, then huffed, and finally released a garbled growl as his body shifted into something larger. Something darker. Something far more formidable.

"There you are," she murmured. Emotion suddenly overcame her, and she launched herself into his ghoul arms and held on tight around the waist, burying her head into the ragged clothing barely covering his chest.

He released a long, labored breath as if the transformation had taxed him. "I was always here with you." His gentle hands smoothed down her hair, much of which had escaped her bun hours ago.

"But Claude is—"

"—is still me. Just the less informed half of me."

"Because he can't remember his ghoul transformation." Her face heated when she realized she'd kissed Claude, and it had been Jack the entire time. Or the other way around.

Jack—no, Claude—no, Jack—answered with deep, rumbling laughter, the sound shaking against her ear. "We are one person. *I* cannot remember my ghoul transformation in my human form. It makes for a…complicated situation."

She lifted her head from his chest to look him in the eye, but she never released him. "Is there a way to help you remember?"

"I don't know."

Then she jabbed an accusatory finger into his chest. "You owe me several apologies and an explanation."

He snatched her hand and lifted it to his lips, giving her fingers a slow, loving kiss. "I was trying to protect you. To tell you as little as possible. It shouldn't have come to this." He sighed. "But I will tell you everything. I promise. Or rather, what I haven't said already. You now know pretty much the entirety of it, minus a few minor details."

"What do I call you, then? Jack or Claude?" Because she was still having a hard time wrapping her mind around the fact that they were the same person.

"Claude is my name."

"It's not very ghoul-like."

He snorted and gently chucked her chin. "Call me whatever you like. I'll always answer."

Somewhere down the hallway, a door slammed, and the sound reverberated against the stone walls surrounding them. It was nearly time to enact their plan. But first...

"How did the vampires not learn of your human identity when they first captured and turned you?"

"My body stays a ghoul when overly distressed. They didn't find out because I never transformed back. At least until I was safe."

"Why not use that other ghoul's blood? The one that turned you."

He grimaced. "Because I killed him to protect myself. Now there is only me." He grinned. "Didn't Claude tell you?"

She gave him a dead stare. "You conveniently left that out."

"Because it happened when that part of my mind was unconscious. Claude wasn't aware. Jack was."

She rubbed at her temples. "You are giving me a headache. Well, the vampires likely know your identity now."

"Perhaps. I don't believe they are aware I can shift. None of them came in to check."

"You're sure?" Because she could have sworn to have felt at least one pair of eyes on her all night.

"I'm sure. Now let's hurry. The night slowly approaches, and you won't have Jack for very long."

She nodded her head. "I'm ready."

Claude lay on the ground, his body and breath eerily still. Her heart stuttered with momentary panic as she waited for even the faintest inhale. It didn't come. He wasn't dead. She *knew* he wasn't dead. But seeing him like this was still disconcerting.

"Somebody help!" she screeched. "He touched the bars!"

A door banged open, and three vampires swooped into the dank room on silent feet. They took one look at Jack, and they, too, seemed a bit panicked like herself.

"He's not breathing," she gasped, letting out a bit of a sob to seal the performance. "He has no pulse."

One of the vampires nodded toward the man closest to the door. "Find Ferdinand. If the ghoul dies, his blood will be no good anymore. He needs to be informed of this development immediately."

The man disappeared from the room in a cloud of foggy smoke while the other two approached the cell. Not a single key jangled against another as one of them unlocked the door, a stark contrast against the squeal of the metal door opening.

"Uhhh," the man said, eyebrows furrowed as he nudged Jack with his foot. "This doesn't look good. Where's that serum?" he asked the other. "It should work momentarily."

The second vampire reached into his pocket and pulled out a syringe needle filled with bubbly yellow liquid. He stooped to inject it, but before he managed the feat, Claude moved so swiftly that even a vampire couldn't counter his attack as he swept the man's legs out from beneath him. The man landed on the floor with a thud.

Clara watched the quick fight with a mixture of dread and fascination. Using his claw, Claude ripped his left arm open, and within skin and muscle and blood lay a silver dagger, hidden inside his own body to avoid detection. He jammed the dagger into the felled vampire's chest. The second vampire gasped, eyes wide as he scrambled to escape. But just as he started transitioning into smoke, Claude grabbed him by the throat and finished him off with the same bloody silver dagger as before.

She breathed heavily despite exerting no energy, staring back at Jack as he stood ripped and bleeding and tall and strong, holding that dagger in his hands.

He huffed and rolled his eyes. "You do realize your fascination with the macabre is disconcerting."

"So you've said before."

His lips twitched, fallen vampires forgotten as he grabbed her by the hand. "Stay close to me. Those vials of my blood are nearby. I can smell them."

"And what about Mazie? We can't just leave her here."

As they traversed down a dark hallway that smelled like mildew and still water, he glanced over his shoulder at her with a regretful expression. "She made her choice. What more can you do?"

Deep down, Clara knew Claude was right. She knew she could do nothing to change things. But her stubborn spirit refused to back down. If she found an opportunity to drag her sister away from this pit of vampires, even kicking and screaming, she silently promised to take full advantage.

Along the way, they encountered a few more vampires. Claude took them down with his silver dagger, and after that, they quickly wised up. Many fled from his path of carnage. Others made themselves scarce.

Their footsteps slowed, so quiet that she wondered if even a vampire couldn't detect them. He led her around a few more corners before they entered a room filled with beakers and vials, bubbling liquid, syringes, and other scientific equipment. Even as a nurse, Clara had no idea what a few of these things were. Her curiosity probed, she approached a beaker suspended a few centimeters over a small flame. Black liquid bubbled within, giving off a metallic stench that seared her nostrils with a single exhale.

"Careful," Claude murmured, guiding her to a safer distance with his arm. "Breathing it in may not infect you, but I don't want to take the chance."

She nodded and watched as he began throwing beakers to the ground and smashing vials of black blood against the wall. Glass shattered. Tables toppled.

Clara couldn't help but find fascination in the way the spikes on Claude's back elongated in his chaotic destruction, the way his sharp teeth snapped and snarled, the way the large muscles in his arms and legs flexed with each table flipped and instrument destroyed.

She bit her knuckle, attempting to maintain a passive expression even when she found his strength beyond impressive. He could likely carry her on his shoulder with ease. He could probably carry *fifteen* of her and hardly break a sweat.

Something grabbed her from behind, startling a gasp from her mouth. "Claude!" she screamed. She attempted to spin around to punch her attacker, but they held on tight. Panic burst to life in Claude's eyes, but he only managed to take a single step forward before something sharp stung her neck.

Dizziness poured through her mind. Her legs became weak. And then her bleary expression spotted the glass syringe sticking out of her body, the last of black ghoul's blood entering her bloodstream.

"Clara!" Claude shouted, but he stopped in his tracks when the vampire holding her threw the syringe to the floor, breaking the glass, and pressed a knife to her throat instead.

"On your knees!" Ferdinand hissed near her ear, his voice sounding far away when her mind continued to sway with disorientation. "Or you will lose that which is most precious to you."

Claude's upper lip lifted as he growled. His knees hit the ground with a thud, his claws flexing with fury.

Ferdinand laughed. "I had hoped it wouldn't come to this, but somehow, I knew it would. You just can't help yourself. Dirtying your hands for *the greater good*. And look where your efforts have landed you." The vampire grabbed Clara's hair and ripped her head back until she whimpered. "You get to watch your pretty nurse turn into the very thing you've strived to keep off the streets."

"Let her go!" Claude begged. "Give her an antidote. I'll do anything. My life is yours."

"There is no antidote. I *want* ghouls on the streets. Why would I bother with an antidote?"

His grip on her hair tightened. Another whimper escaped her mouth.

A gasp on the other side of the room pulled her attention to the familiar silhouette of her sister.

"You promised you wouldn't hurt her!" Mazie screeched. She tried to rush forward, but Ferdinand threw Clara to the ground, grabbed Mazie, and trapped her arms to her sides with his own arms wrapped around her. She kicked and struggled, but the other vampire proved much stronger than her. "You promised!"

Ferdinand laughed. "Do you know how politicians get to the top, dear? By spewing promises they can never deliver. I need the ghoul to know *we* are in control. To break him at the very beginning to get him to comply. The perfect tragedy."

"But she's my sister!"

"And you helped turn her in. You are as much to blame for what happens as myself."

Clara pushed herself to her hands and knees, wincing when glass cut into her skin. She still felt dizzy, and her scalp burned from mistreatment, but there were no other side effects thus far. When would she become a ghoul? How long did it take?

On the opposite side of the room, Claude released a pained grunt. Clara's eyes darted in his direction only to find his body shrinking little by little until his human form replaced the hulking mass of ghoul. Daylight hadn't come yet! She briefly wondered if one of these deadly concoctions in the room was influencing a premature shift.

His hand rested against his temple, his eyes unfocused as he glanced from person to person in the room. His attention lingered longest on Clara's neck on the spot of blood dripping from a syringe wound.

Anger contorted Claude's expression. He pushed himself to his feet and flew at Ferdinand in a rage. The vampire side-stepped easily and kicked Claude's bad leg. He collapsed, unable to walk far without his cane to aid him.

"What have you done to her?" he hissed.

But Ferdinand only grinned in fascination. "Things are starting to make so much more sense! You can shift? Into the police detective at that. No wonder you kept slipping through our fingers. I never could have guessed."

Clara lifted her hand to her neck and touched the wound. According to news articles and police reports, the deaths happened quickly. That meant the infection also spread quickly if Claude took care of it so fast. Currently, she was showing no signs of infection. No inflamed or swollen skin. No pain. No pus or liquid other than blood escaping the small wound.

As a nurse, she would have given it more time just to make sure. But also as a nurse...

She believed she was *not* infected. Did this mean she was immune?

She glanced toward Claude, eyes wide. It was almost as if he understood her fleeting look across the room. Perhaps... Perhaps, as another conjecture, she might be immune because of her connection with Claude, with the ghoul. They were mates, body and soul. Was that protecting her? It made far more sense than just luck. Working in medicine, she didn't believe in luck. Only science. And this hypothesis was better than anything else she might be able to come up with on quick notice.

Ferdinand shoved Mazie aside and approached Clara with a frown. "It should have happened by now... No matter. I have many ways to use you to get the ghoul to comply."

The vampire reached out a hand toward Clara, and she knew right then that she was useless against a vampire far faster and stronger than herself. Any attempt to fight would be futile. But that didn't mean she wouldn't try.

She reached for the scalpel in her pocket, holding it tight in her hand. She was not about to comply without a good fight.

"Don't hurt her!" Mazie released an ear-splitting screech as she moved forward, nearly faster than Clara's eyes could follow. Her sister grabbed Claude's silver knife and jumped onto Ferdinand's back.

Ferdinand attempted to throw her off, but whenever Mazie was determined to do something, nothing could stop her. Not even a strong, wily vampire.

With another inhuman screech, Mazie plunged the silver dagger into the man's neck. Only then did he manage to grab a hold of her and throw her off him. Like a cat, she flipped through the air and landed on her feet, bracing herself as if readying herself for more fight.

But Ferdinand was preoccupied with the knife in his neck. Smoke wafted from the weapon. A burning stench filled the air. The vampire grabbed the knife and pulled it out, throwing it aside. It clattered against the ground and skittered beneath a table.

However, the damage was already done.

Smoke continued to burn through his neck. The acrid stench became stronger by the second. Clara covered her nose with her hand, but it did nothing to block out the smell nor the vampire's screams of agony as the silver from the weapon coursed through his blood. It only took a short time for the silver to circulate through his body. The man's flesh burned from his bones, quickly followed by his skeletal structure, until nothing remained but a pile of ash.

An eerie silence descended upon the room as Clara's mind tried to catch up with the most recent events. When her brain finally reacted, she glanced around in a panic. All vampires had fled the scene, none seeming to dare to make themselves known. Claude was on his hands and knees, panting against what was likely the exhaustion caused by his shift. And Mazie…

She was untouched. Her red eyes transitioned back to their regular blue hue as if her vampire instincts sensed an end to the danger.

The two sisters stared back at one another for a long moment. She wasn't sure who moved first, only that they threw their arms around each other and hugged the other tight.

"Please forgive me," Mazie cried, her face buried in her shoulder. "This was never supposed to happen. I thought this was the right thing to do."

"You did not come this far without good reason and great hardship." She squeezed her sister in a tight embrace. "I hold no ill will against you."

"Thank you," Mazie sniffed. "I only wanted out of this terrible city. I don't know what to do now."

Claude stepped forward in his ragged clothing, exhaustion boring a hole into his entire demeanor from the dark circles under his eyes to the slump in his shoulders. "I believe I can help with that. You and Norma will come to live with me and

Clara in Paris." He turned to Clara and clasped her hands between each of his. "If you will have me."

"I'm not going anywhere without you," she replied in a breathy whisper. "Perhaps I'll get a real shot at becoming a doctor. One with an actual degree."

He laughed and kissed each of her hands. "A bit of warning, dove. The deal comes with a ghoul on the side."

She grinned. "Even better."

"Claws, tail, and sharp teeth included."

She enjoyed the thrill of the warning. "I look forward to it."

"And a bit of monster hunting with the detective career."

She tugged only one hand away to place it on her hip. "Are you trying to scare me away? Because it's not working."

"I'm only trying to see how far you will go for me."

"All the way."

"All the way," he murmured disbelievingly before tugging on her hand and pulling her into a kiss.

She instinctively melted against him, the heat of his kiss both smoldering with heat and icy with pure relief. She was glad he was safe. She was relieved they'd all made it out of this situation alive, even if it wasn't the outcome she'd expected. Now that mysteries were revealed, and pieces of the puzzles put together, her decision was easy.

Yes, she would go wherever he did. Two people joined body and soul. Her mate. Her rock. Her heart's desire. Her Claude.

"I think I'll just..." Mazie hummed awkwardly. "Umm...make myself scarce."

She and Claude broke the kiss to laugh as Mazie crossed the room to observe something on the wall with an overly intense expression.

"Does this mean you remember everything?" Clara asked, searching the blue of Claude's eyes.

He nodded. "I remember everything. Even in this form now. The moment Ferdinand turned to ash, I remembered."

"This was not how I envisioned things panning out. She ran a hand down the length of Claude's arm.

He grinned, his "kiss with a demon" pulling his mouth on one side. "No. It's better."

And then he pulled her into another kiss, and she knew without a doubt... This was where she always wanted to be.

Chapter Sixteen

It was brighter in Paris.

It was almost as if a fog had lifted from the skies, as if the darkness that had plagued Whitechapel no longer held her within its grasp. Paris had afforded her opportunities she'd never thought possible, especially with Claude as her source of constant support. He'd believed in her. And now?

The fruits of her labor stood before her as she stared at her new clinic bathed in sunset gold, surrounded by colorful trees beginning to transition to red and yellow with the turn of the autumn weather.

After a couple of years of schooling at Faculté de Médecine de Paris, she was now officially able to call herself a doctor, all thanks to Claude, who had graciously paid for her education. His generosity had opened opportunities she'd only dreamed of her entire life. Although she had been one of the few women attending, she looked forward to proving that a woman could also receive the same education as a man and forge a path in the medical world.

Just like her father.

Oh, she truly hoped he was proud of her, smiling down at her from heaven.

Now, she was a doctor with a clinic of her own. A clinic with a catch…

A grin stretched across her face as she glanced first at Mazie and then at Claude as they gazed at the structure before them in awe. A real clinic with beds and equipment and plenty of space for patients.

And it even included a separate, private clinic in the back for paranormal patients. The non-evil ones that Claude *didn't* hunt, of course. He wasn't entirely thrilled with the idea, knowing how dangerous the paranormal could be, but he'd allowed her to pave her own path, and she couldn't be more grateful to her mate.

"This isn't how I imagined getting out of Whitechapel," Mazie commented as she sidled up to one side of her, remaining within the shadows of a tree to protect herself from the waning sunlight. "But it's far better than the alternative."

"You mean the part where you become a vampire spawn?" Clara teased.

Mazie flashed her fangs at her and rolled her eyes. "I'm stronger in this form. I will not be taken advantage of again. Therefore, I do not regret my choice."

Clara reached out with one hand and squeezed her fingers sympathetically while squeezing Norma's fingers with her other hand. "This is a new start for us. No matter how different we'd imagined our own futures."

"The darkness isn't so bad. It's full of new people and waiting adventures."

She squeezed Mazie's hand again. "It sounds like a good opportunity for you."

"And I get to help in the infirmary," Norma chipped in with excitement in her voice. "I'd like to be a nurse. Maybe even a doctor one day."

Just like Father.

With a light laugh, she gave her youngest sister an encouraging squeeze around the shoulders. "The doctoring itch must run in the family."

Her searching gaze found Claude leaning on his cane near the corner of the clinic where the autumn foliage brushed against the glass of the small greenhouse on the side of the building. He gestured with his head for her to follow him.

As her sisters argued about the ethics of vampires, she slipped away into the shadows and rounded a large tree to find Claude leaning against its trunk, his hat resting on top of his head. A grin played at the corners of his mouth as he reached for her hand and pulled her closer. He kissed her fingers, her wrist, and then explored her jaw with the light trace of his lips.

A sigh escaped her at his gentle, loving touches, and he quickly muffled the sound with his lips against hers. She was powerless against the warmth of his body, the strength of his hands as he pushed her against the tree and trapped her wrists above her head.

"You didn't just call me over to kiss me senseless," she breathed between heated kisses, wrapping one of her knees around his leg.

"And if I did?"

She giggled as his nose skimmed against the ticklish spot on her throat. "Then you must really like me."

"'Like' is a vast understatement, dove." He lowered her left hand from the tree and kissed her knuckle right above where her diamond ring resided on her finger. They'd married within a week of first arriving in Paris, and she wouldn't have had it any other way. "I think the right word might start with an 'L.'" He pulled her flush against him and kissed one corner of her mouth. "Followed by an 'O.'" He kissed the other corner. "'V.'" And then he hovered just over her mouth, his minty scent tantalizing and filling almost every corner of her mind.

"'E,'" she finished for him, grabbing a fistful of his suit and pulling him into another breathtaking kiss. She threaded her fingers through the soft blond strands of his hair and took the kiss deeper, wanting to taste every inch of his mouth and feel the heat of his body mingle with hers.

"Be careful," he murmured against her lips. "The Ripper is about to emerge, and he won't want to show any mercy."

"Is that a threat?" she whispered, eyes glazed over with desire. "Or a promise?"

According to officials, the Jack the Ripper case was thrown out the window, deemed unsolvable much to the frustration of police and detectives everywhere. The Whitechapel murderer had taken no more victims, as was included in official police reports. But unofficially, Claude's ghoul blood was no longer out there, no longer a threat.

He was free from danger. And she hoped things would stay that way.

"Let's find out, shall we?"

The last rays of sunlight descended below the horizon, bathing the city in a quiet dusk. The muted blues and oranges momentarily drew her gaze to the beautiful skies hovering over Paris. And when she returned her attention to Claude…

Yellow eyes gazed back at her. Clawed fingers took her hand and kissed her from finger to wrist. Pointed teeth peeked out from a grin. It was their little secret. One she would keep for the rest of her life.

Time for MORE Monsters? Check out the rest of the Time for Monsters series below!

Time for Monsters Series Page
https://www.amazon.com/dp/B0DH2RSZR2

A Victorian Demon's Guide to London, Love, and Being a
Hero
S.C. Principale

Seduced in Sleepy Hollow
S.C. Principale

Clutching Cthulhu's Pearls
Marilyn Barr

Rise of the Gods: Vandon's Destiny
Bella Blair

Seduced by the Shedu
Roslyn St. Clair

A Mermaid's Tail
Danielle Sibarium

Shiver Me Satyr
Marilyn Barr

Taken by the Ripper
Sydney Winward

Unwrapping His Mummified Heart
Roslyn St. Clair

ABOUT THE AUTHOR

Sydney Winward is an award-winning fantasy and paranormal romance author who dabbles in the occasional historical fiction. She loves building complex worlds filled with magic, strong characters, and emotional stories.

Sydney is the author of the Sunlight and Shadows Series and the best-selling Bloodborn Series, and when she's not writing, she's reading, thinking about stories, or going on adventures with her children. She lives in Utah with her husband and three amazing kids.

www.sydneywinward.com